## "It's time we became lovers, Amber."

Gray's tone was sensual, his eyes gleaming with hunger. He pulled her into his arms.

"If you're sure," she ventured, even as she reveled in the strength of his hard body.

"I'm sure all right." He buried his lips in the vulnerable hollow of her throat. "You're so soft and warm and exciting. I don't know how I've waited this long."

Exquisite relief permeated Amber's heady excitement. The waiting was over! Tonight the marriage would begin for real. . . .

**Jayne Ann Krentz** doesn't claim to be a poet, but the verses she wrote for *Between the Lines* show originality and whimsy. Writing good poetry is difficult, she reports—writing deliberately bad poetry is almost impossible!

Jayne is one of the top-selling romance authors in North America, with more than forty books to her credit. She also writes as Stephanie James and Jayne Castle.

## Books by Jayne Ann Krentz

### HARLEQUIN TEMPTATION

### HARLEQUIN INTRIGUE

These books may be available at your local bookseller.

Don't miss any of our special offers. Write to us at the following address for information on our newest releases.

Harlequin Reader Service
901 Fuhrmann Blvd., P.O. Box 1397, Buffalo, NY 14240
Canadian address: P.O. Box 603,
Fort Erie, Ont. L2A 9Z9

# *Between the Lines*

## JAYNE ANN KRENTZ

# *Harlequin Books*

TORONTO • NEW YORK • LONDON
AMSTERDAM • PARIS • SYDNEY • HAMBURG
STOCKHOLM • ATHENS • TOKYO • MILAN

Published October 1986

ISBN 0-373-25225-0

Printed in Canada

## 1

CORMICK GRAYSON TOSSED ASIDE the handful of papers he'd been going through, poured himself another dash of cognac and said calmly, "It occurs to me there's no good reason why we shouldn't get married."

Amber Langley choked on the sip of elegant cognac she had just taken. "I beg your pardon?" She gasped for breath as Grayson lightly slapped her between the shoulder blades. It was a friendly gesture, just the sort she would have expected from him. He was, after all, her good friend. "What did you say?"

"You heard me." Grayson gave her his slow, fleeting smile, the one that only briefly revealed his strong white teeth. His hazel eyes were gently amused as he lounged back against the black leather cushion of the sofa. "I can't think of a single good reason why we shouldn't get married. We're friends, we work well together and you're practically living here in my house as it is."

Amber blinked, trying to regain her equilibrium in a world that seemed to have tilted an inch or two. "Practically is a long way from actually," she managed to point out a little dryly. "I work for you, remember? You choose to run your business from your home. That makes your house my office. What it really amounts to is that I'm spending a lot of time in the office these days, Gray."

He shrugged, his massive shoulders moving with careless ease beneath the fabric of the conservative white shirt he wore. "You don't seem to mind the time you spend here."

"No," Amber admitted thoughtfully. "I don't mind the time I spend here." She studied him closely. Cormick Grayson was a large specimen of masculinity. There was no fat on him, but there was a sure, solid strength in the broad shoulders and strong thighs. Everything about him seemed oversized, including his hands and feet. Amber estimated his height as slightly over six feet.

His hazel eyes were a cross between green and gold. There was a direct, watchful intelligence in his gaze that Amber occasionally found disconcerting but never really unnerving. The rest of his features were just as straightforward, from the firm line of his mouth and jaw to the bold blade of his nose. Grayson was nearly forty, a powerfully built man whose face echoed that power. His hair was a deep shade of brown that contained the faintest hint of russet. It was thick, and Grayson kept it severely trimmed. He wore his hair as conservatively as he wore his clothes.

For all his size and sleekly muscled build, Cormick Grayson was a quiet man. He spoke softly and moved silently. It was precisely that element of quietness coupled with strength that Amber found so appealing. Grayson wasn't flashy, unsettling, temperamental or unpredictable. He was calm, thoughtful, easygoing and pleasantly predictable. *Placid*, was the term Amber's sister Cynthia used.

Amber had noticed most of Cormick Grayson's reassuringly placid qualities in almost the first moment she had introduced herself. That had been nearly three months ago when the temporary secretarial help agency had sent her out on assignment to his house. He had greeted her at the front door of his lakefront home just outside of Bellevue, Washington, with a politely appraising expression in his hazel eyes. He'd shaken her hand in a no-nonsense manner, introduced himself as Cormick Grayson and then instructed her to call him Gray. When she'd told him her name was Amber, he'd seemed genuinely amused by the fact that they both bore names related to colors.

Amber knew she probably hadn't impressed Grayson with her passable but somewhat limited secretarial skills. Typing was hardly her forte. Like many other women who found themselves temporarily out of work in their areas of expertise, Amber had fallen back on her basic ability to type. As she had told Cynthia, it was either that or wait tables until she was able to land a job in her field.

But two weeks into the assignment with Gray he had offered her full-time employment as his assistant. Her typing wasn't anything special, he'd told her, but she had a head for business. It was not an altogether surprising discovery. Until recently Amber had worked in a high-powered advertising agency in Southern California. Among other skills she had an instinct for handling clients and an intuitive feel for business situations. She knew how to generate enthusiasm with a smile, a talent Gray found quite fascinating and useful in dealing with his clients.

And, perhaps most importantly, she didn't mind helping him with his research on the little known Western poet Sherborne Ulysses Twitchell. Amber was secretly convinced that it was her tolerance on the latter subject that had got her the job offer. Not many people were inclined to be tolerant of the work of S. U. Twitchell. Amber had accepted the position as Gray's assistant at once.

Tonight Grayson was offering marriage in the same casual, reasonable manner in which he'd offered Amber a job. Cormick Grayson did everything in a quiet, reasonable, unflamboyant manner. It was one of the things Amber appreciated about him. Nevertheless, the marriage proposal managed to take her by surprise.

"You're serious, aren't you?" she asked.

"Very. It makes sense, Amber. We work well together, we respect each other, we enjoy each other's company. Our goals and interests are similar. I want you to give the matter serious consideration." He smiled self-deprecatingly. "I know I'm not the most passionately exciting man on the face of the earth, but you don't seem to be looking for passion or excitement."

Amber shook her head quickly, her eyes earnest. "No," she whispered, "you're absolutely right. I'm not looking for either." She'd had far too much of both six months ago with Roarke Kelley. The extreme highs and the equally extreme lows of her relationship with the championship race car driver had kept her off balance for two months before she'd finally pulled herself together long enough to put an end to the destructive whirlwind. Kelley had brought passion and fire and romance into her world on a scale that was larger than life. Amber had learned the hard way that she wasn't the kind of woman who was cut out to cope with the turmoil such extremes of emotion caused.

She had fled Southern California and the excellent job with the advertising agency in search of a more stable, more serene existence. She had decided to visit her sister's family in Bellevue and had wound up staying. Amber had found exactly what she was searching for when she'd gone to work for Cormick Grayson. Gray was right. The kind of marriage he was offering was precisely the type to which she was most suited. But there was a little matter of honor and integrity.

She didn't love Gray.

She liked him, admired him, respected him, but she didn't love him. Amber sometimes wondered if her ability to respond to love and passion had been forever destroyed by the fires of her involvement with Roarke Kelley.

"Tell me what you're thinking, Amber." Gray didn't move from the corner of the couch as he watched a myriad of expressions cross her face.

Amber was the perfect name for her, Gray had often thought. It accurately described the brown-gold of her hair and the warm color of her faintly slanted eyes. The hair was worn in a mass of small curls held back from her face tonight by tortoiseshell combs. The halo of golden brown framed the wide, heavily lashed eyes, a full mouth and a delicately shaped nose and chin. Amber was an intelligent woman with the sort of face people found interesting, even attractive, but not particularly beautiful.

In the nearly three months he had known her, Gray had never seen her wear much makeup. That suited him just fine. But it also made him curious. He wondered occasionally how much makeup she had worn when she'd worked as an account executive at the advertising agency in Southern California. Something told him that her severe restraint with eye shadow, blusher, lipstick and nail polish now was another of her reactions to the life she had once known.

She dressed well, although the colors she chose tended to be subdued and conservative. Gray was willing to bet she hadn't worn those colors in the flashy environment of California advertising. He thought she would look good in vivid reds, yellows and greens, but most of her wardrobe had proven to be in muted shades. Gray liked her best in jeans and an open-throated shirt such as she had on tonight. It seemed to him that her true nature was more revealed in such casual attire.

Regardless of what she wore, he was always pleasantly aware of the delicious curve of her small breasts and the provocative roundness of her well-shaped derriere. Lately it was getting almost impossible to keep his hands off her. She was not a dieting zealot and that pleased Gray. He had no particular fondness for fashionably skinny women. He didn't know many men who did. As Sherborne Ulysses Twitchell had once said in a line from one of his more inspired verses, "a woman should look like a woman, not a starving heifer." As devoted to S.U.T. as Gray was, he couldn't remember how the next line went. Twitchell had not been able to find anything memorable to rhyme with heifer. Nevertheless, it was the thought that counted, and Twitchell's thoughts on the matter of the feminine shape equated nicely with Gray's. A man could enjoy a good meal with Amber and not have to watch her pick delicately at her food.

A man could enjoy a lot more than his food with Amber Langley, Gray knew. There was a warm, sweet passion in her that was just waiting to be tapped. At the moment it was still hidden safely under wraps. Gray was almost certain that it was concealed not only from most of the people who met Amber, but also from

Amber herself. Some man in Southern California had singed her badly. She needed time and peace in which to recover. But Gray had determined within a day or two of meeting Amber Langley that when she was prepared to explore her emotions again he was going to be the man in the vicinity. If he talked her into marrying him, his position would be more or less assured. He would be standing in front of Sleeping Beauty when she awoke.

From beneath half-lowered lids that concealed the watchfulness in his eyes, Gray waited for Amber to answer his question.

"What am I thinking?" she repeated with a faint frown. "Just that you've taken me by surprise. I hadn't realized—" She broke off to run her tongue nervously over her lower lip. "I hadn't been aware that you were viewing me as a . . . a wife."

Gray smiled gently. "Why not? I think I know you fairly well after these past couple of months together. What more could I want in a wife?"

Amber took a firm grip on her resolve. "How about love?" she suggested baldly. "Gray, I'm very fond of you, but I don't love you. I'm not sure I'm capable of loving a man, at least not in the fiery, passionate way men always seem to want."

"Do I strike you as the fiery, passionate type?" One dark brow lifted in sardonic amusement. "How strange. I always think of myself as placid and quiet. Definitely a slow burner."

In spite of her mixed emotions, Amber found herself grinning. "You have no idea how comfortable it is to be around a slow burner."

"Then marry me and be comfortable on a full-time basis."

Amber's smile faded. She looked down at the glass of cognac cradled in her hands. "Are you sure you know what you're doing, Gray?"

"Have you ever known me when I didn't know what I was doing?" There was no arrogance behind the remark. Cormick Grayson always knew what he was doing.

Amber was aware of that. She shook her head. "No, Gray. I've never seen you make a serious mistake, at least not in business. But this is a little different, don't you think? This is marriage."

"What's so different about marriage? I've analyzed the situation and us. I think we'll be good together. Neither of us is the hot-blooded type. We aren't blinded by a lot of emotional garbage and we're both basically honest. Furthermore, I think we're both capable of making a commitment and sticking to it. What more does it take to make a marriage work?"

Amber moved one hand in an exasperated motion. "What more? I don't know what more it takes, Gray. I've always heard it takes love and passion in addition to integrity."

"Don't you believe it. A lot of successful marriages have taken place during the past few thousand years, and I'm willing to bet that almost none of them were based on love and passion. The truth is, the twentieth-century notion of romantic love is a fairly recent development. No one during the past few centuries expected to marry for love."

Amber's head came up, her eyes narrowing faintly. "I know. Previous generations married for money or business reasons or to beget heirs. None of those reasons apply in this case. I'm quite capable of supporting myself, there's no overriding business reason to marry you and unless you've suddenly decided you need an heir, I don't see what—"

Gray grinned briefly at the stubborn look on her face. "Calm down. I was just trying to point out the fact that a marriage doesn't have to be forged in the fires of a volcano in order to be successful." He held up one large palm as if to forestall any further protest. "There's no need to argue about it. I'm certainly not going to push you into anything. You know me better than that. All I ask is that you think about it. And don't worry about not being able to offer me some fantasy of passionate love. I don't expect it and probably wouldn't know what to do with it if I got it."

Amber relaxed, her mouth curving slightly. "You sound like quite an authority on the subject."

He shrugged again. "Maybe I am. I was married once. For about two years. That was a long time ago, back when I still worried about things like fiery passion."

"I didn't know." Amber was suddenly intensely curious, but she didn't dream of prying.

"It's been over a long time. I learned a lot, Amber. Believe me, I know what I'm doing this time." He sat up and placed his snifter down onto the glass-topped end table with careful precision. "I'm not going to rush you for an answer, although I'll admit it would be convenient for us to get married within the next couple of weeks."

"The next couple of weeks!" Amber was startled.

"I have to leave for Arizona at the end of October. You know that," he reminded her gently. "The Symington deal."

"Oh. Yes." She frowned. "But what's that got to do with us?"

"I just thought the trip would make a pleasant honeymoon."

"Honeymoon." Amber felt dazed.

"It's customary, you know."

She glared at him briefly. "I'm aware of that."

"It wouldn't have to be the usual kind of honeymoon, Amber," he said meaningfully. "I meant what I said. I'm not going to push you in any way. But I am going to be stuck spending a week or ten days at a very posh dude ranch and I thought you might enjoy enduring the hardship with me. Just think. We could see the very kind of desert landscape Twitchell mentioned in 'Gunslinger's Lament.' Perhaps stand on the very rock Red Bart hid behind when he ambushed the U.S. marshal in 'An Ode to Badlands and Bad Men.' It's the literary chance of a lifetime. You'll be able to combine a vacation with a dose of culture."

Amber stared at him for a few seconds and then collapsed into laughter. "Culture is not exactly the word I would use, but I see your point. I think you're trying to bribe me, Gray."

"Of course I am. The trip would do you good and I would very much like to have you along. As my wife, not just my assistant."

Amber sobered again and ran her finger around the edge of the snifter she was holding. "I don't know, Gray. I honestly don't know. I'm very honored and flattered that you're asking me to marry you, but to tell you the truth I haven't given much thought to marrying anyone. At least not recently."

He reached out to stroke his thumb along the line of her jaw. His eyes were gentle with understanding. "I know. And I meant what I said about not rushing you. But think about it, Amber. It would be convenient to be married before the Arizona trip, but if that's pushing it I'll be glad to wait. I really am quite sure of what I'm doing."

Amber was aware of a deep tension coiling within her. "You honestly wouldn't expect a wild, intense kind of love from me, Gray? Because I don't have it to give. And you're too nice a man to have anything less than what you want. I'd like you to be happy."

"You can make me happy, Amber."

"You're very sure?"

"Very sure."

"I'll . . . I'll think about it," Amber whispered.

"TO TELL YOU THE TRUTH, Cynthia," Amber stated the next day as she sat in the passenger seat of her sister's BMW, "I'm actually considering his proposal."

"I can't believe he made such a casual thing of it. For Pete's sake, it sounds as if he asked you to marry him the same way he might have asked you to type one of those reports he's always doing for his clients." Cynthia Paxton slipped the car into a turn lane with unerring accuracy. She was driving toward the huge indoor mall that covered a large chunk of downtown Bellevue real estate. Cynthia could probably have driven the route from her home to the shopping center blindfolded. She spent a lot of time at the elegant mall; many people in Bellevue did.

Cynthia was two years older than Amber. Her short, sassy, stylish hair was a few shades darker than her sister's, and she had inherited their father's blue eyes instead of the golden-brown ones Amber had been endowed with. She had been working in the personnel department of a Seattle bank when she'd met and married her husband Sam. Sam Paxton was a successful stockbroker. Cynthia had quit her job shortly before her son Drake was born, intending to go back to work when Drake turned three. In the meantime she had taken to the life of the affluent suburban matron like a duck to water. She also took her duties as an older sister seriously. She was free with advice.

Amber threw Cynthia a wry smile. "If I'd given the matter any thought, I would have guessed that Gray would have asked a woman to marry him in exactly that manner. It's just his style. He's a quiet, calm, deliberate sort of man."

"Dull is the word you're looking for," Cynthia said. She spun the wheel of the BMW, pulling into the large parking complex that surrounded the mall. She began cruising between the lanes of parked cars. With an expert's eye she perused the aisles of already tethered BMWs, Volvos and assorted Japanese-made vehicles. "Placid, dull, nice and boring. Are you sure that's what you want, Amber? Just because he looks like a quiet port after the storm of Roarke Kelley, don't jump into anything. Things may have ended badly with Roarke, but that doesn't mean you'd be happy with someone who's his direct opposite. After all, when you were happy with Roarke, you were *very* happy. Almost euphoric."

"And when I was unhappy I was absolutely miserable," Amber concluded firmly. "I can do without the highs I had with Roarke, Cynthia. They aren't worth the price. The last thing I want is another situation such as the one I had in California. The truth is, I really think I might be quite content with Gray."

Cynthia slipped into a parking space and switched off the ignition. Turning in her seat, she slanted an assessing glance at her sister. "Is content going to be enough, Amber?"

"I'm almost certain it will be for me," Amber said slowly.

"But?"

"But I'm worried that it might not be enough for Gray. He deserves more, Cynthia. He's a good man. He deserves someone who really loves him."

"And you don't."

Amber sighed. "I like him. I'm comfortable with him. I respect him. But I don't feel anything as strong as a grand passion for him. I don't think I'll ever feel that way about anyone again. I got burned out on Roarke."

Cynthia tapped one crimson nail against the steering wheel, ignoring her two-year-old son who was starting to bounce up and down in his car seat and make anticipatory noises. "Tell me something, Amber, how do you feel about Gray as a lover?"

Amber flushed slightly, surprised to find herself more flustered by the question than she ought to have been. "I'm not repulsed by him, if that's what you mean."

"That's not what I mean. Are you attracted to him? Has he kissed you? Have you been to bed with him?"

Amber yanked at the door handle. "No, I have not been to bed with him. Not that it's any of your business."

"Amber, you're talking about marrying the man. You've got to consider the physical side of things."

"He's kissed me a couple of times," Amber muttered as she opened the car door and got out. She didn't add that the kisses had been brief, casual and friendly rather than passionate.

"Kissed you a couple of times! My God, what a Romeo. Be still, my beating heart." Cynthia opened her own door and then reached into the back seat to remove Drake from his car seat. "You've been practically living in his house and all he's done is kissed you a couple of times?"

"I have *not* been living in his house. I work there." It annoyed her that Cynthia had made virtually the same observation Gray had made about the situation.

"Relax," Cynthia said in the soothing way older sisters have of calming their younger siblings. "I just meant that there doesn't seem to be much excitement involved here."

"There isn't," Amber agreed. "I like it that way."

"And so does Gray? You're sure of that?"

"He says he's quite satisfied with the arrangement. He made it **very** clear he won't rush me into anything."

"What do you call rushing? He wants you to marry him in less than two weeks!" Cynthia exclaimed.

"Only because it would be convenient." Even as she said the words, Amber experienced a sense of chagrin. It was true she didn't want a wild, flaming affair, but Gray's approach to the matter did sound a little prosaic. Surely even a quiet, placid marriage should be scheduled for reasons other than convenience. In the next instant she determinedly banished the thought. Convenience was as good a reason as any for the scheduling of a wedding.

"Tell me something," Cynthia challenged as she led the way toward the mall entrance, "does Grayson get excited about anything?"

"Well, there is Sherborne Ulysses Twitchell," Amber murmured with a hidden grin. "There have been moments when Gray has become positively exhilarated by the subject."

"Twitchell! That idiotic nineteenth-century poet Grayson claims to have discovered?"

"Twitchell's for real," Amber assured her. "Gray's got three copies of the collected works of S. U. Twitchell. All privately printed and signed by the great man himself. As far as Gray knows, they're the only copies in existence. That makes Gray the official expert on the guy."

"It's crazy. When you first told me about the whole thing, I thought it was a joke. There are times when I still think it is."

Amber shook her head. "It's no joke. Gray's had several articles on Twitchell published in some obscure little poetry newsletters. He had a rather interesting piece hit print a couple of months ago."

Cynthia shot her sister a suspicious glance. "Really? What magazine?"

"A small one called *Radiant Sunsets*. It's a monthly devoted to the history of Southwestern poetry. Gray's article was entitled 'The Desert as a Metaphor for Psychic Isolation in the Works of S. U. Twitchell.' I helped him write it."

"Good grief, you don't have to sound so proud of the fact."

"It's kind of fun," Amber said with a bashful grin. "I enjoy arguing with Gray on the subject. Twitchell is such an incredibly bad poet."

"Does Grayson acknowledge that?"

"Are you kidding? He'd defend Twitchell to the last literary ditch."

Cynthia shook her head in exasperation. "I can't believe you're thinking of marrying a man who's so utterly boring that the only thing that excites him is the analysis of a terrible poet no one else has ever heard of.

For heaven's sake, Amber, think about what you're doing."

Amber shoved her fingers into the front pockets of her jeans as she followed her sister into the bustling mall. "I have thought about it. And the more I think about it, the better it sounds. If Gray is sure he'll be satisfied with a woman who isn't passionately in love with him, then I believe I'll say yes." She was aware of a curious satisfaction as she reached her decision. "I think I will be quite content with him."

Cynthia groaned. "Well, you're a grown woman. You have to make your own decisions. What about this matter of having to get married in two weeks? What's the rush, anyway?"

"Gray has a consulting assignment down in Arizona. One of his clients is considering buying a fancy dude ranch down there. He wants Gray to look over the operation and give him an opinion."

"Grayson gets a hefty fee for his business consultations, doesn't he?" Cynthia noted shrewdly.

Amber shrugged. "He does all right."

"Sam checked him out, you know."

Amber glared at her. "No, I didn't know. When was this?"

"Back when you first went to work for Grayson. Don't look at me like that. I was worried about you. You seemed to be functioning in a daze when you first arrived from California. You had just quit a high-paying, fast-lane ad job and you were about to go to work as a temporary secretary, for goodness' sake. Two weeks into that job and you quit to go to work full-time for some guy who's so low-profile he doesn't even maintain a proper business address. Naturally I was concerned. So I asked Sam to make a few inquiries. He did and came up with the news that while Cormick Grayson operates in a discreet manner doing these financial consultations for his clients, he seems to be successful. His business reputation is sterling."

"I could have told you that," Amber muttered. "Gray is a very honorable man. His word is his bond. He's kind of old-fashioned in that respect."

"I'm sorry for interfering, Amber," Cynthia said gently, "but I really was worried about you."

Amber took a deep breath and let it out slowly. "I know. It's okay, Cynthia. I understand. If the situation had been reversed, I probably would have done the same. Roarke went through my life like a whirlwind. When it was over, I probably didn't appear to be acting too rationally for a while. But that's all in the past now."

"Are you sure? It seems to me you're still letting that relationship affect the way you behave. Would you be seriously considering Grayson's proposal if you hadn't had that brush with Roarke Kelley?"

Amber tried to come up with a reasonable answer and was startled to discover she couldn't. "I don't know," she admitted honestly. "If I hadn't met Roarke, I might be a different person now. But I did get burned by him and it did change the way I think about relationships."

"Are you positive you're not turning to Gray on the rebound?"

Amber shook her head. "I'm not on the rebound. I wouldn't go back to Roarke under any circumstances And I wouldn't ever want to marry anyone like him." She took a deep breath. "Cynthia, I've made my decision."

"I can see that," Cynthia said quietly. "No more sisterly lectures. Just remember that if it doesn't work out, you're not trapped for life. You can always file for divorce."

Amber looked away uneasily, not liking the all too practical words of wisdom. "I know. Let's not talk about it anymore, Cynthia."

"Just be sure you invite me to the wedding, regardless of how small it is."

"Consider yourself invited."

THE NEXT MORNING Amber used her key to let herself into Cormick Grayson's home at the usual time. He had given her the key shortly after she'd started working for him. The house was a strikingly modern structure built with walls of windows to take advantage of the view of Lake Washington. The interiors were influenced by the serene Japanese style of design. Allowances had been made for American notions of comfort and for Cormick Grayson's size, but a tranquil, clean-lined look had been achieved. Amber liked the house very much. She stood for a moment on the sleek hardwood floors of the expansive living room and admired the view.

"Is that you, Amber?" Gray called from the kitchen.

"Unless you've given a key to someone else," she retorted lightly.

Gray appeared in the wide doorway that separated the dining area from the living room. He was carrying two cups of tea. "No one else has a key," he told her gently. "You know that."

"Ummm." Feeling unexpectedly nervous all of a sudden, Amber went toward him to take one of the mugs of tea. "Then it must be me."

"Brilliant deduction. Did you make your decision?" Gray asked blandly.

Amber's fingers trembled slightly as she gripped the mug. There was no reason for this attack of anxiety, she told herself. Cormick Grayson was hardly the sort of man to inspire anxiety of any kind. The man had simply asked her to marry him. It was quite obvious that for him the matter was no big deal, so why on earth was she getting nervous? Amber summoned a smile. "You're absolutely positive this is the kind of marriage you want, Gray?"

His hazel eyes were half concealed behind lazily lowered lashes. "I'm positive."

Amber took a deep breath. "Then, yes, please, I would like to marry you. Thank you for asking me."

He took a sip of tea and studied her over the rim of the mug. His hazel gaze was unreadable, but when he lowered the cup there was a faint curve edging the hard line of his mouth. "Thank you for accepting. I'll make the arrangements this afternoon. You don't mind if we keep it very small?"

Amber shook her head, wondering why she felt a vague sense of disappointment. Surely she hadn't been expecting anything more than a quiet, businesslike acceptance of her answer. "I'd prefer to keep the wedding small. I'll only be inviting my sister and her husband."

"Fine. We'll take them out to dinner after the ceremony." Gray took another sip of tea, his expression thoughtful as though he were already working through the details in his mind.

Impulsively Amber touched his sleeve. "I'll try to be a good wife to you, Gray."

He smiled, but his eyes were still gleaming with an unreadable emotion. "I know." He hesitated and then said very seriously, "I'll do my best to be a good husband to you, Amber."

She looked up at him searchingly, uncertain of what she should say or do next. It was all very well to talk about a passionless arrangement, but somehow this quiet discussion of such a major event was a little too placid. "Gray. . ."

He lowered his head and brushed her mouth lightly with his own. The brief caress was warm and affectionate, but not much else. Amber closed her eyes, and her fingers tightened on the sleeve of Gray's shirt until she could feel the sinewed strength of his arm. She didn't know what she expected or even what she wanted. Amber just knew she wanted more than the light, meaningless kiss she had just received.

She felt Gray go still for a moment and then very carefully he removed the mug of tea from her hand and set it down beside his on a nearby table. Without a word he pulled Amber into his arms.

# 2

AMBER WENT INTO THE EMBRACE with a sense of curiosity and mild trepidation. She just didn't know what to expect, either from him or from herself. But she discovered immediately that she needn't have worried. What she found in Gray's arms was a warm, comforting strength that seemed to enfold her completely. Quite suddenly Amber wasn't sure why she had been at all nervous.

Gray's big hands moved down her back in a slow, stroking motion that compelled her gently against him. Amber leaned into the heat of his large body and lifted her face for his kiss. Gray covered her mouth with his own, moving his lips warmly on hers. He made no effort to deepen the kiss, but seemed content to let her set the pace. Half curious and half relieved, Amber slowly put her arms around his neck. She was vividly aware of the sleek muscles of his shoulders. Unconsciously her lips parted under his.

Gray exhibited little interest in the gentle invitation she had issued. He didn't even touch his tongue to her lower lip, let alone attempt to explore the intimate confines of her mouth. But he seemed willing to let Amber become familiar with the feel of him. When her fingertips sank gently into the skin of his shoulders, however, Gray sighed lightly and slowly lifted his head. He smiled down at her.

"I think everything's going to work out fine," he declared calmly.

Amber tilted her head slightly, strangely disturbed by the sensual curiosity she had begun to sense within herself. She regarded Gray with grave uncertainty. "You meant what you said about not rushing the . . . the physical side of things?"

"Amber, have you ever seen me rush anything?" he asked with a disarming smile.

She had to laugh. "Sorry I asked." She stepped back. "Well, I guess we ought to start work or something." She struggled briefly and found her composure. "I'll take a look at the mail."

"All right. I'll join you in the office in a few minutes. I want to grab some data sheets I was working on in the kitchen." Gray turned away to saunter casually back through the wide doorway as if nothing of any great moment had just occurred between himself and Amber.

Amber was surprised to find herself wondering irritably how many times Gray had asked a woman to marry him. He seemed awfully casual about it. But as quickly as the thought surfaced, she dismissed it. Cormick Grayson was acting exactly as he always did. Calmly unflappable, placidly confident. She smiled to herself and headed for the large study that Gray called his office.

The day's mail was sitting on her desk. Gray had brought it in earlier, and as usual, he hadn't bothered to go through it. He left that chore up to his assistant. Amber sat down at her desk in front of the floor-to-ceiling windows and picked up her brass letter opener.

She was halfway through the pile of advertisements, bills and business letters when she spotted the familiar return address on a long manila envelope. Amber grinned and instantly slit the flap. A two-page letter signed by one Honoria Tyler Abercrombie fell into her hand. She began reading it at once.

"What's that?" Gray asked as he strolled into the office and glanced over her shoulder.

"A letter to you forwarded by *Radiant Sunsets*." She glanced up at him. "It's about the article you did for the newsletter a couple months ago. Remember? The one on the desert as a metaphor for loneliness. You used 'Gunslinger's Lament' as an example."

"Ah, yes," Gray said in satisfaction. "One of my better pieces, if I do say so myself. 'Gunslinger's Lament.' Who can forget such classic lines or such an unusual sense of poetic meter." Before Amber could halt him, Gray began to quote:

"He dreams of her at midnight
When there's no one else around.
He sees her in the morning's light
When he wakes on the cold, hard ground.
But he knows he'll never touch her,
He knows she'll never care.
She's his sweet, illusive vision,
The lady with the golden hair."

Amber rushed to interrupt him before Gray went into the next stanza. Once started on a Twitchell poem, Gray was hard to stop. "Well, it seems as though your article generated some feedback from a reader named Honoria Tyler Abercrombie."

Gray's eyebrows rose. "Feedback? My articles never generate any feedback. No one else knows enough about S.U.T. to argue with me."

Amber waved the letter in her hand, her eyes glinting with amused satisfaction. "Looks like your claim to being the world's only living expert on Sherborne Ulysses Twitchell is about to be challenged. Ms Abercrombie, here, says she has a copy of the *Collected Works* plus several handwritten pages that appear to have come from a diary kept by Twitchell."

Gray looked stunned. He snatched the letter out of Amber's fingers. "Impossible. I've got the only three existing copies of the *Collected Works*. And as for a diary of Twitchell's, that's utter nonsense. Abercrombie must be a fraud."

"I don't know, Gray. She seems to have a firm grasp of her subject."

"Probably gleaned from reading all my articles," Gray snapped, scanning the letter with a glowering frown. "Listen to this, Amber, the woman has the nerve to claim she's going to publish an article next month in *Radiant Sunsets*."

"What topic?"

"'The Use of Erotic Metaphors in the Poetry of S. U. Twitchell.'"

Amber chuckled. "I know exactly what she means. Just think of all those references to hot iron and cold iron and heavy iron in his stuff. Definitely phallic. There's that line in 'Gunslinger's Lament,' for instance." She paused and then quoted:

"She was satin, lace and elegance;
He was leather, sweat and iron."

Gray shot her a disgusted look. "Iron is a slang term for a gun."

"Everyone knows guns are phallic symbols for men."

"Hah! That's a typically female thing to say."

Amber looked offended. "I happen to agree with Ms Abercrombie. It's not as if I'm unfamiliar with the poem. Listen to this:

The lady came from Boston,
He heard them call her Sharon.
She was on her way to 'Frisco
To marry a cattle baron.
The gunman saw her in the depot;
She came within a foot of him that day.
And he held his breath as she did pass and
Her skirts did gently sway.

She was satin, lace and elegance,
He was leather, sweat and iron.
But as she passed her glance did chance
To fall upon his face.
She looked into his night-dark gaze and
Saw his destiny so clear
That in her soft blue eyes there formed
A single, crystal tear."

Gray leaned against Amber's desk and finished the poem with the reverent appreciation of a true aficionado:

"But the lady didn't turn away;
The lady didn't run.
Instead she left him with a smile
That was like the morning sun.
Yes, she smiled at him with kindness;
She smiled at him with grace.
The gunman knew he'd ne'er forget

Her sweet, angelic face.
He knew then he'd never hold her,
Knew then she'd never care.
But he also knew he'd ne'er forget
His lady with the golden hair."

Amber grinned and reached out to tap the letter in his hand. "Looks like you've got some competition, Gray. There is now another Sherborne Ulysses Twitchell expert in the world, and she's gunning for you."

"I'll demolish her in print. I'll show her up for the fake she is. I'll see to it the woman is laughed right out of *Poets of the Southwest*, *Western Poetry* and *Radiant Sunsets*. Just wait. The phallic symbolism of iron, my foot. Abercrombie obviously doesn't know what she's talking about."

"It'll be interesting to read her article," Amber said politely.

"It'll be a joke, mark my words." Gray got to his feet and stalked over to his own desk. He threw himself into the swivel chair and regarded his assistant with a dangerously narrowed gaze. "This Abercrombie female has bitten off more than she can chew. I'll make her eat every word she gets into print."

"Now, Gray, she's probably a sweet little old lady. An ex-librarian, perhaps. Someone who is as devoted to S.U.T. as you are."

Gray gave her a scornful glance. "A sweet little old lady who's writing an article on the phallic symbolism of guns and who knows what other erotic metaphors? Hah. Forget sweet little old ex-librarian. Whoever this woman is, she's obviously got her mind on something besides the unique literary qualities of S.U.T.'s poetry."

He sat forward and reached for a file labeled Symington. "Let's get busy. We've got work to do."

Amber stifled a laughing smile and obediently went back to the mail. So much for the emotional impact of accepting Gray's proposal of marriage, she told herself. Her future with Gray might not be wildly passionate, but it would probably be somewhat amusing at times. And that kiss hadn't been so bad. She was more than willing to appreciate warmth and comfort and strength in a man's embrace after having experienced the destructive flames of a lethal passion.

THE MORNING OF AMBER'S WEDDING dawned overcast and drizzly. She dressed for the event with a sense of uneasiness that she couldn't quite shake. There had been nothing very abnormal about the past two weeks. Gray hadn't changed his behavior in any way. There had been a few brief, affectionate kisses but nothing more intense, not even a repeat of the pleasantly comfortable embrace he had given her the day she'd accepted his proposal.

He'd announced a few days before the wedding that they would be married on the same day they were scheduled to leave for Tucson.

"It'll mean we'll be taking your sister and her husband out to brunch instead of dinner, but I don't suppose that makes any difference to them," Gray had remarked.

Amber had shaken her head. "No, I don't suppose it will," she'd agreed politely.

It was all so terribly casual, she thought as she slipped into the skirt of the apricot-colored suit she'd bought for the event. Of course, she reminded herself, casual was the way she wanted it. But still, it seemed to her that a wedding, any wedding, ought to warrant more than a short, businesslike ceremony followed by breakfast with the family. The flight to Tucson that afternoon was fundamentally a business trip.

But she didn't want the customary romantic trappings, Amber told herself fiercely as she combed her hair back from her face and inserted a silver comb behind each ear. She was not the usual bride who had her head filled with romantic nonsense and a body eager to taste the sensual delights of the marriage bed. She wasn't in love with Cormick Grayson and probably never would be, at least not in the way most people thought of love. Roarke Kelley had cured her of those dangerous, risky passions.

But she would be content with Gray, Amber knew. Her life would be serene and quietly satisfying on several levels. Gray was making a commitment this morning, and she knew him well enough to know he would abide by it. She, too, was capable of honoring a commitment, and she fully intended to honor the one she was making today.

Amber knew she could do without the kind of painful, passionate yearning that left a woman so terribly vulnerable. She collected her small tan leather purse and headed for the door of her apartment. Cynthia and Sam Paxton were due to pick her up at any moment.

GRAY STRETCHED HIS LONG LEGS out in front of him and held out his hand for the cup of coffee the hostess was offering. The drone of the jet engines was a distant hum up here in first class. He almost always flew first-class on any trip scheduled to last over an hour. It was the only way he could get a seat with enough leg room. The extra space was the only real advantage of first class as far as he was concerned. Free liquor didn't mean much, and the food really wasn't any better than that served in the other cabin, even if it did arrive on prettier china. But he was willing to pay the premium for a measure of extra comfort.

Besides, he reminded himself, this was his wedding day. He wanted his new bride to enjoy the trip in comfort. He smiled to himself. Amber was getting a kick out of flying first-class. So far she had sampled every freebie offered by the attentive air hostess, including the imported champagne.

Gray studied his bride surreptitiously as she polished off the last of the chocolate cheesecake that had followed the steak. She hadn't eaten very much at the bountiful hotel brunch after the short wedding ceremony. He was glad to see her normally healthy appetite returning. She seemed to have relaxed somewhat since her sister had bid her goodbye at the airport. Gray had a hunch Cynthia Paxton had made one or two last-ditch efforts to talk Amber out of the marriage.

But now Amber appeared to be returning to her natural, even-keeled mood. He wondered how she'd behave this evening when she realized the sun was setting on her wedding night. Gray thought he knew Amber quite well, but there were still times when he couldn't tell what she was thinking. Today was one of those times.

His own thoughts were the ones he should be trying to unravel, Gray decided wryly as he took a swallow of coffee. He'd changed his mind at least half a dozen times already this morning on a very important subject. In another half hour he'd probably change it again. The vacillation disturbed him. It wasn't like him to be so unsure of himself.

The raw truth was that he didn't know how to handle the wedding night that was rapidly approaching. He'd awakened this morning with an aroused body and the last vestiges of an erotic dream that involved Amber shimmering passionately in his arms. As he'd climbed out of bed and headed for the shower, Gray had been absolutely certain of what he'd be doing on his wedding night. The hell with waiting, he'd told himself. He'd been waiting for months.

But during the small, private ceremony in the minister's office this morning he'd looked at Amber's sweetly earnest expression and decided he could wait a little longer to have her in his bed. He didn't want her coming to him out of a sense of wifely duty or obligation. He didn't want to make her nervous or uncomfortable. He didn't want to rush her. Gray wanted Amber to want him with the same abiding desire that flowed in his own veins for her.

The noble sentiments had suffered a serious setback at brunch when Amber had looked at him across the table and smiled. Amber's smile had a way of temporarily depriving him of his breath. There had been a mysterious gleam of emotion in her expressive eyes, and for an instant Gray had dared to hope that she had faced the prospect of the coming night and found it exciting. But the expression had disappeared beneath a mask of good-natured politeness that had lasted all the way to the airport. Gray had changed his mind at least three more times before the plane had left the ground.

He took another sip of coffee and scowled. It was ridiculous. He was nearly forty years old, and as of today he was a married man. The woman sitting beside him was no ingenue who had been swept off her feet by a dashing, older man. He might be a few years older than Amber, Gray told himself with ruthless honesty, but he definitely wasn't dashing.

No, Amber had married him with her eyes wide open. She had done so after spending almost three months getting to know him, working with him, learning his moods and temperament. She knew what she was doing, or at least she thought she did. That last notion sent a prickle of guilt through Gray.

He immediately squelched the niggling, uneasy sensation. After all, she certainly hadn't married him under duress, Gray thought. And she was a woman of integrity and honor. She would fully expect to fulfill her wifely duty tonight. There was even the possibility that deep down inside she might be looking forward to fulfilling that duty. Whether she wanted to admit it or not, there was a sensual side to her nature.

There was absolutely no reason he couldn't take his wife to bed tonight, Gray decided. She would come to him willingly; she would be expecting to share a bed. She might even enjoy it. Damn it, he would make certain she enjoyed it.

But, then again, he thought stoically, it would be so much better if she came to terms with her own buried passion first. It would be so much more satisfying if she acknowledged to herself that she truly wanted her husband and didn't simply feel an obligation to let him exercise his conjugal rights. He reminded himself that he had never intended to try shaking Sleeping Beauty awake. He'd simply intended to be standing in front of her when she finally opened her eyes.

Gray's fingers tightened around the cup in his hand. He had thought things would get simpler once he'd convinced her to marry him. Now he wasn't so sure.

"There's a lot to be said for flying first-class," Amber announced with unabashed enthusiasm as the plane set down on the runway in Tucson. "We even get to exit the plane first. No standing around in the aisles waiting for the crowd ahead of you to move. Do you always fly this way?"

Gray smiled briefly. "Whenever I can write off the trip as a business expense, I do."

Some of the pleasure faded from Amber's smile. She felt the expression on her face turn polite. It was a little disconcerting to know that your wedding trip was being written off as a business expense. Still, she couldn't deny the practicality of the matter. And this was hardly meant to be a dazzlingly romantic honeymoon. The Symington deal was the most important element of this vacation.

"My God, it's bright out here." Amber blinked in amazement a short time later as she and Gray walked out of the terminal and found the waiting limousine with the emblem of the resort on its doors. "And so warm."

"You've lived too long in the Northwest," Gray said. "You've already forgotten what real sunlight is like." He glanced toward the distant foothills of the mountains that encircled Tucson. The desert valley was domed with an endless lid of blue sky. "Sort of puts you in mind of one of S.U.T.'s memorable lines from 'The Long Ride South,' doesn't it?"

"I feel a quote coming on," Amber observed.

"Of course you do. This is Twitchell country. Being here is bound to bring out the urge to cite his work." Gray paused dramatically and then recited in suitably somber tones:

"He galloped south to the border
Trapped in the heat of the desert sun.
His brain was filled with a dangerous rage,
He was an outlaw on the run."

Amber nodded thoughtfully, watching as a smiling, suntanned young man got out of the limousine to greet them. "There were some phallic overtones in 'The Long Ride South,' as I recall. Something about 'The big iron on his thigh.' It'll be interesting to see if Honoria Tyler Abercrombie mentions it in her article next month."

"You and Ms Abercrombie seem to have phallic images on the brain," Gray remarked.

"Pure literary observation," Amber assured him. She broke off to smile pleasantly at the sandy-haired man walking toward them. He wasn't dressed in the normal chauffeur's outfit, she noticed. His head was bare, and he wore a short-sleeved, brightly patterned shirt, jeans and a pair of running shoes. He had an engaging, open smile and seemed to know it.

"Afternoon, folks. My name is Ozzie. You're the Grayson party?" He looked at Gray with polite inquiry.

"That's right. I'm Cormick Grayson and this is my wife, Amber."

Amber was rather startled to hear the satisfaction that underlined the word *wife*. But there was no time to dwell on the significance. Sandy-haired, blue-eyed, smiling Ozzie was already shaking hands and collecting baggage. A moment later Amber found herself settled beside Gray in the back seat of the limo. Ozzie slid into the driver's seat and turned the key in the ignition of the big car.

"I'll have the air-conditioning going in a minute," Ozzie promised cheerfully. "You folks been to Tucson before?"

"Yes," Gray said absently.

"Well, I haven't," Amber announced. "If you're about to give us a travelogue, feel free. I'll listen to every word."

Ozzie laughed. "It's either that or I'll turn on the stereo. We've got a long trip ahead of us."

"Where are we headed?" Amber asked.

"Into the foothills of those mountains you see in the distance." Ozzie launched into an entertaining monologue that covered everything from pointing out the peaks in the Santa Catalina Mountains to a lecture on the distinctive, candelabra-shaped saguaro cactus.

Amber listened attentively, aware that Gray seemed to be dwelling on private thoughts. Probably already tuning his mind to the business that lay ahead of him, she decided, surprised by the faint disappointment she felt. This was, after all, primarily a business trip for him. She mustn't forget that.

The resort Gray's client was considering buying was an impressive, majestic structure perched in the foothills of the even more majestic mountains. It was a considerable distance from the sprawling suburbs of Tucson. The architecture was a modern interpretation of the Spanish style that was so evident in Southwestern buildings. The hotel wings extended on either side of a stunning, three-story glass-and-stone lobby. As Ozzie turned off the main road and up a wide drive, Amber saw the entrance to an extensive, wonderfully green golf course. On the other side of the drive several tennis courts were being utilized by players in perky little outfits. There was also a riding stable available, Amber knew, and a large pool.

"Welcome to the Inn of the Desert Flame, the most complete resort in the Southwest," Ozzie said with a proud grin as he slid the big car to a halt in front of the lobby. "Everything you want or need is available on the premises. Three restaurants, a lounge, shops and a friendly staff. Enjoy your stay. Mr. Delaney will be glad to know you've arrived."

Amber leaned close to Gray and asked in a low whisper, "Who's Mr. Delaney?"

"Victor Delaney is the owner. He's the one trying to sell the place to Symington's group of investors." Gray stepped out of the limo and reached back inside for Amber's hand. "Things have changed since Twitchell's time." He glanced around at the opulent resort.

"Thank heavens," Amber murmured as she slipped out of the car to stand beside him. "I think I prefer my desert complete with indoor plumbing, swimming pool and air-conditioning."

Just then the glass doors in the lobby entrance slid open and a tall, slim, balding man in his late forties strode forth with an extended hand and a ready smile. Everyone seemed to smile a lot around here, Amber thought.

"Glad to see you, Mr. and Mrs. Grayson. I'm Vic Delaney. I hope you enjoy your stay." Delaney shook hands with the enthusiasm of a professional host, but there was no doubt about the genuineness of his greeting. He, too, was tanned and wore a sporty short-sleeved shirt. But instead of jeans he had on a pair of expensive, casual slacks. He wore white leather moccasins and a matching white leather belt. There was an air of exuberant vitality about him that was meant to be contagious. Amber had frequently met his sort in the advertising world. It was obvious Vic Delaney had been in the resort business a long time. "I certainly hope you find everything in order. The staff is anxious to please, so feel free to call on anyone at any time. I'm looking forward to doing business with you, Cormick."

"Call me Gray." Gray accepted the handshake with a polite nod. Then he slid a hand possessively under Amber's arm. "My wife and I are looking forward to our stay."

"Right this way," Delaney said, leading them into the lobby. "I'll have someone show you to your rooms at once." He nodded toward another sandy-haired, tanned young man in a short-sleeved shirt. "Roger, these are the Graysons. I've already taken care of the paperwork. Show them upstairs, will you? One of the bellboys can bring the luggage later."

"You bet, Mr. Delaney. Right this way, please." The young man named Roger came forward with alacrity.

Perhaps there was something in the desert air that bred this particular species of tanned, sandy-haired young specimen of manhood, Amber thought as she and Gray followed Roger to the elevators. Roger and Ozzie could have been twins. Both appeared to be in their late twenties and both appeared to spend time working out in a well-equipped gym. They were lean and fit and strongly muscled at the shoulders, and they smiled a lot.

Roger chatted with them in the elevator, asking the usual polite questions about their flight. Amber did most of the answering. The young man seemed to bore Gray. She slid a sidelong glance at her new husband as she stepped out of the elevator and into a carpeted hallway. Gray had not only slipped into one of his quiet

moods, he had also gone a little grim. Amber wondered what he was thinking.

A moment later blue-eyed Roger threw open the door
of a suite at the end of the hall, and Amber stopped
worrying about whatever it was that was preoccupy-
ing Gray.

The suite was beautiful. It had a fabulous view of the
desert valley on which Tucson sprawled. Carpeted in a
rich forest green, it was furnished in a delightfully cool
tropical style that was very inviting when set against
the desert backdrop outside the windows.

And it had two bedrooms, one on each side of the
cozy sitting area. *Two bedrooms*.

Amber took a deep breath, wondering at the implications of a two-bedroom suite on a honeymoon. Had
Gray actually requested two bedrooms or had friendly
Vic Delaney simply given them the best room in the
house and it happened to have two bedrooms?

Amber stood in the middle of the emerald-green carpet and stared blindly out at the spectacular view while
smiling Roger gave Gray a rundown on how to operate
the air-conditioning system and how to summon room
service.

By the time she heard Roger's cheerful farewell and
sensed the door closing silently behind him, Amber had
one of her own bright smiles fixed firmly in place. She
swung around to meet Gray's intent, unreadable hazel
eyes. "It's certainly a lovely room, isn't it? I think I'll
make it a point to travel with you frequently on your
business trips in the future."

"I'm glad you like it." Gray paused, glancing at the
twin doors that led to the bedrooms. "Puts me in mind
of another verse from Twitchell."

"I don't think I want to hear it," Amber informed him tartly. She was remembering the article Gray had published on Twitchell's use of the desert as a metaphor for isolation and loneliness. She wasn't sure if Gray had been about to quote one of Twitchell's maudlin verses on loneliness or not, but those were certainly the lines this suite brought to her mind. "I'm going to take a shower and change into slacks and sandals."

Gray nodded, loosening his tie. "Okay. I think I'll go downstairs and let Delaney show me his office and introduce me to the staff who handle the books I'll need to look at while we're here."

"Books?"

He nodded. "The *financial* books. I'm supposed to be here on business, remember?"

"I remember," Amber whispered. She turned away and started for the plush bathroom.

"I'll have the bellboy put your luggage in the right-hand bedroom when he gets here, all right?" Gray called after her.

Amber couldn't tell if there was a faint note of challenge in his voice or not. Was he asking her whether she expected to have her own room or was he telling her? "That will be fine, Gray."

Amber fled into the bathroom.

# 3

AMBER FELT SHE HAD REGAINED both her emotional equilibrium and her sense of perspective by the time she and Gray finished dinner in the beautiful hotel dining room. The wine Gray had ordered with the meal had no doubt contributed to her relaxation, she decided with a small smile.

Outside the dining room windows, subtly directed lighting illuminated a huge, multileveled terrace that contained gardens, a magnificent swimming pool and two or three smaller wading and spa pools. The mountains rose steeply behind the resort, their peaks clawing a star-filled sky. It was a dramatic setting.

Amber had tried to dress for the setting and the evening. She was wearing a sheath of emerald-green silk that was a bit brighter than her normal attire. It was, in fact, a dress left over from her California days. She had kept it because she had never worn it around Roarke. It was, therefore, not imbued with painful memories.

Gray had seemed a little surprised when she'd appeared dressed for the evening, but his eyes had been appreciative as he took in the sight of the green silk, her delicate high heels and the elegantly neat twist of her hair.

"I'm having a hard time believing I'm married to you," he'd said with a curious curve of his mouth.

"I know what you mean." Amber had answered with an attempt at a light, careless laugh. She could hardly take her eyes off him. Dressed in an immaculate light gray suit, he seemed very tall, very solid and powerful. When he had taken her arm shortly before dinner to guide her to the elevator, she had been more than usually conscious of the strength in his large hands.

All day long Amber's mind had been playing with sensual images conjured up by her vivid awareness of Gray's quiet strength. She had rerun the memories of his brief, casual kiss so many times in her head that she had every nuance memorized.

She still didn't know if he'd arranged for the two-bedroom suite or if it had just been a fluke that they'd received it. But she did know that after her luggage had been deposited in one room Gray's suitcase had been taken to the other. The question of where he would choose to sleep tonight was haunting her now that the evening was progressing inexorably to a close.

"This resort seems quite isolated," she ventured in a deliberately conversational tone as the waiter removed the last of the dishes. "Does Symington realize just how far this place is from town? The mountains start right there outside the window."

"The isolation is supposed to be part of the charm," Gray told her. "People coming out West to a fancy dude ranch want the feeling of being really away from civilization."

"As long as they have all the amenities at hand," Amber added with a grin.

"Naturally. When you pay a mint for a few days in the desert, you want your money's worth. Like Ozzie said, this place offers everything you could want plus a nice feeling of getting away from it all."

Amber leaned forward, not wanting her voice to carry. "Symington's group of investors is going to have to spend a fortune if they want to buy it."

"Symington's investors have a fortune to spend. And they will if they think the deal is sound."

Amber didn't need to be told that it was Gray's job to give his opinion on the soundness of the deal to Symington and his people. "How did the books look this afternoon?"

"I barely got a chance to find out where the accounting office is located," Gray said dryly. "Delaney spent most of the time giving me a pep talk on his resort. But I've arranged to sit down with the accountant and the head bookkeeper tomorrow morning."

"Will you need me?" Amber heard her own words and was oddly embarrassed. "Tomorrow morning, I mean?"

He didn't seem to have picked up on the sexual innuendo in her words. "No, I don't think so. It will take me a while to get oriented." Gray looked at her as he signed the dinner tab. "Would you like to dance? There's a trio playing in the lounge."

"Yes," Amber said, smiling brilliantly, "I'd like that very much."

In the glass-roofed lounge, Gray started to take Amber's hand with a cool formality that sent a shaft of uneasiness through her. She looked up at him, her eyes filled with silent questions. He studied her face for a moment in the soft light and then he opened his arms. She walked into them without any hesitation at all.

Amber could feel the warmth in his big hand as it pressed against the small of her back. His other palm enfolded her fingers. Gray drew her close against him, silently inviting her to put her head on his shoulder.

With a small sigh, Amber accepted the unspoken invitation.

"Do you realize this is the first time we've ever danced together?" she murmured.

"I realize it." His fingers tightened briefly around her hand, and he inhaled the fresh, clean scent of her hair. "I think we fit together very nicely."

"Yes," she agreed. "We do." *Perfectly* was the word she would have used to describe how well they went together on the dance floor. She couldn't help but wonder if they wouldn't fit together just as perfectly in bed. She nestled a little closer and was happy when Gray's arms tightened around her.

It amazed Amber to find her mind so filled with erotic images tonight. Two weeks ago when she had listened to Gray's casual proposal she had been certain that the most she would ever feel for him was a pleasant, comfortable affection. But the sensual pictures dancing through her head tonight went considerably beyond pleasant, comfortable or affectionate. And the heat that seeped into her bloodstream as Gray drew her more deeply into his hard strength was also several steps beyond anything generally implied by those three bland terms.

A tiny, jarring jolt of deep awareness went through Amber as she abruptly realized that she was on the verge of feeling more than she had wanted to feel. More than she had ever *expected* to feel toward Gray.

She lifted her head from his shoulder and looked up to find him watching her face. His hazel gaze was almost gold in the soft light of the lounge. His mouth was edged with the faintest of smiles. Gray didn't miss a beat in the smooth rhythm of the dance, but Amber knew he had realized something was wrong. She summoned a small, uncertain smile in an attempt to assure him that there was nothing to be concerned about. Desperately she searched for a casual conversational gambit.

"The resort seems to be well run, Gray. It's crowded and the grounds appear well kept. All in all it has the look of a successful operation."

He shrugged. "Things aren't always as they appear on the surface."

She knew instinctively he wasn't referring just to the operation of the resort. Unable to think of any brilliant comebacks, she simply nodded as if in agreement and kept her mouth shut for the remainder of the dance. But she didn't put her head back down on his shoulder.

It seemed to Amber there was a new and subtle tension in the atmosphere surrounding Gray and herself. She wasn't quite sure when it had first appeared. It was as if it had crept up on them, gently enveloping them without any warning. She had known Gray for three months, long enough to become comfortable in his presence. Indeed, she couldn't remember ever feeling uncomfortable around him.

But tonight she was more vividly aware of him than she had ever been in the past. Aware of the clean male scent of him. Aware of the gold in his hazel eyes. Aware of the strength in him.

It wasn't all that abnormal, she tried to assure herself as Gray led her back to the small table they were sharing. After all, this was her wedding night. Even if she wasn't passionately in love with her groom, she was still bound to be very conscious of him. It was idiotic to be feeling so nervous. She had no fear of Gray. He would be a gentle, considerate lover, and the plain truth was she had been quietly looking forward to her wedding night all day.

*Quietly* was the operative word, she reminded herself. She had been quietly, pleasantly, complacently looking forward to her wedding night. She hadn't expected any waves of dangerous excitement or panting anticipation. Furthermore, Amber was fairly certain Gray wasn't expecting anything along those lines, either. She wished she understood why there was a faint trembling in her fingertips when she reached for her glass of after-dinner liqueur.

"It's getting late," Gray observed a few minutes later, setting his glass down on the polished table. "And I've got to meet that accountant and the bookkeeper early tomorrow morning. Ready for bed?"

Amber looked at him from behind a veil of lashes, trying to guess how intimate he meant the question to sound. She nodded politely. He reached for her hand, and a few minutes later they were back at the door of the suite. Amber's palms felt damp as Gray put the key in the lock. It would be easier if he put his arm around her, she thought. It would be a lot easier and simpler if he made the first move. He was the groom. Surely it was his responsibility. It was traditional, for heaven's sake. Amber would have given everything she owned in that moment for a glimpse into Cormick Grayson's mind.

But shortly after they had walked into the green-carpeted room, she realized she didn't need any psychic powers to tell her how the evening would end. Gray casually slipped out of his jacket, loosened the knot of his tie and undid the first button of his pristine white shirt. He smiled at Amber.

"Got everything you'll need in your room? I think the bellboy put the right cases in the right rooms, but I didn't check."

Amber swallowed and summoned up one of her re-assure-the-client smiles. "Yes, I'm sure I've got every-thing."

He nodded. "Then I'll say good night and let you get some sleep." He stepped toward her, dropped a brief kiss on her mouth and sauntered toward his bedroom. "Don't bother getting up when I do in the morning. This is supposed to be a vacation for you."

"I'll keep that in mind." She hadn't realized how cool her words sounded until Gray turned at the door and raised a questioning brow. Hastily Amber dredged up another smile. "Good night, Gray. Thank you for a lovely evening."

"Thank you for marrying me," he said gently and disappeared into his room.

Amber stared after him, confused and more than a little miffed. It was a full minute and a half before she finally realized she was simply standing and staring at a closed door. Irritated not only with Gray but with herself, she deliberately moved toward her own room. When she was safely inside, she shut the door a little too hard and sank down on the bed. Her mind was churn-ing.

*All right,* she thought. *So this isn't the romance of the century. That doesn't mean the bride and groom are supposed to spend their wedding night in separate rooms.*

It wasn't as if Gray was the shy type. He'd had no trouble proposing marriage in the first place. There must be a reason for his behavior.

Amber chewed her lower lip, her mind clicking rap-idly through other reasons why Gray might want to spend his wedding night alone. She got to her feet, kicked off her high-heeled sandals and began pacing the room. The ridiculous part was that she didn't know whether to be offended or hurt or relieved.

Her fingers went to the zipper of the emerald silk dress. She paused to step out of the delicate material. With great care she hung the dress in the closet and reached for the expensive but rather modest pastel peignoir set she had bought for her wedding night. When the gown was firmly sashed around her waist, she stood in front of the full-length mirror and glared at her image.

She was thirty years old. She had married Gray in good faith. She fully intended to live as his wife. If he hadn't intended the same, he shouldn't have asked her to marry him. There was no point.

Fired now by her sense of injured female pride and a desire to settle a matter that should never have become a problem in the first place, Amber walked to her door and flung it open. Then she stalked boldly across the sitting room and knocked on Gray's door.

Several seconds passed before Gray responded to the knock with a deep, rumbled "Come in, Amber."

She opened the door and stepped inside. He was standing at the window that overlooked Tucson. He'd removed his shirt and shoes but still wore his slacks. He didn't turn around as Amber came through the doorway. She found herself captivated by the sleek contours of his broad shoulders and taut waist. It took her a few seconds to find her voice.

"I think we should talk, Gray."

"It's not necessary. Not tonight." His voice was soft but there was an unexpected roughness underlying the words. "Things will work out in time, Amber."

She took a step forward, but he still didn't turn around. "I don't understand. If you don't want . . . I mean if you hadn't intended for us to live together as man and wife. why did you ask me to marry you?"

He glanced back at her finally, startling her with the deep, brooding quality of his gaze. He seemed momentarily absorbed by the sight of her in the nightgown and robe. Then his eyes lifted to her earnest face. His expression softened. "There's plenty of time for us, Amber. I'm in no hurry. I'm not going to rush you."

"You seemed eager enough to rush me into marriage," she couldn't resist pointing out somewhat brusquely.

"The timing was convenient."

"Is that all I'm meant to be to you? Convenient?"

He frowned and swung around completely, striding toward her. "Amber, honey, what's wrong?"

"That's what I'm asking you."

He stopped a foot away from her and tilted her chin upward on the edge of his hand. "We're friends, remember? Not a couple of hot-blooded young lovers who can't control themselves. We'll take this slow and easy. One step at a time."

She ignored that, searching his face intently. "Gray, you *are* interested in women, aren't you? I mean, you didn't marry me just to make your business clients think you're, uh, heterosexual, when you're not, did you?"

He stared at her for a startled moment and then something very warm and brilliant flashed in his eyes. Without a word he pulled her into his arms and kissed her in a way he had never kissed her before.

Amber was so astonished she couldn't move. There was all the familiar strength and warmth she had come to expect in Gray's embrace, but it was as if he'd temporarily removed hidden restraints; restraints she hadn't even guessed existed.

The strength she had always found comforting suddenly became compelling in an elemental, primitive way. It sent shivers through her. The warmth she had hitherto sensed in him was suddenly the first, licking flame of a fire that promised something far more dangerous than blandly pleasant heat. Unconsciously her mouth opened under his, and she felt the sensual touch of his teeth on her lower lip. Gray fitted his large hands around the soft curves of her buttocks and lifted her against him. She was vividly aware of the taut heaviness of his lower body. His tongue flickered across hers, and Amber inhaled sharply. Then she whispered his name in a soft, pleading way. Gray set her down.

Amber's lashes lifted abruptly, her eyes wide and startled as she stepped back and looked up at him.

"Does that answer your question?" he asked in a calm voice that belied the remnants of heat in his eyes.

Amber blinked and nodded once. "Yes," she breathed, "I think it does."

He smiled gently. "Then go back to your room and stop worrying. I told you everything will work out in time."

"But you want me," she whispered uncertainly.

"I can wait."

She stared at him, perplexed. "For what? Gray, I'm thirty years old. You don't have to treat me as if I were a naive teenager."

He gave her a crooked, wry grin. "I have a hunch most teenagers are a good deal less naive than you are, Amber."

"What's that supposed to mean?"

He sighed. "Honey, I told you I'm willing to wait."

"But I'm not asking you to wait. I'm your wife. I married you fully expecting to share your bed."

"You still don't understand, do you?" He stalked slowly back toward the window, his gaze on the distant lights of the city. "When you come to my bed, Amber, I'd like it to be because you genuinely want to be there, not because you're feeling obliged to do your wifely duty."

Flustered, Amber felt an awkward warmth infuse her cheeks. She was glad Gray was looking out into the night instead of at her. Quickly she regained her self-control. She cleared her throat and said staunchly, "Gray, I think I would like to share your bed. It seems the perfectly natural thing to do under the circumstances. I don't mind doing my duty. Honestly I don't."

He swung around at that, his face a mask of cold, male anger that took her completely by surprise. She had never seen Gray lose his temper. She'd never seen him behave in any other way except in a calm, placid, thoroughly *safe* manner.

"Go back to your room, Amber. I told you we'll take this slowly and I meant it." There might have been anger in his eyes, but his voice was still perfectly calm and controlled.

An unexpected fury swept through Amber. It surprised her, arising as it did out of nowhere and taking her by storm. "Damn you, Gray, I don't know what you think you're waiting for! I married you because I thought we understood each other. I assumed we thought alike on the subject of sex. I expected to share a mature adult relationship with you. You knew I wasn't some kind of hot-blooded, passion-starved sex kitten. If you thought I'd turn into one after you married me, you made a colossal mistake!"

"Did I?" But his anger was already fading. Unfortunately for Amber's mood, however, Gray's temper was giving way to a masculine amusement that further infuriated her.

"Yes, damn it, you did!" She lifted her head proudly and marched out of the room. The door slammed loudly behind her. When she took her fingers from the doorknob, she discovered she was shaking. Stifling a sob, she fled into the safety of her own bedroom and locked the door.

Gray stood alone in the middle of his bedroom and contemplated the recently slammed door. For a moment his face was expressionless and then a slow smile curved his mouth. His hot-blooded, passion-starved sex kitten had just discovered her own claws. With any luck it wouldn't be long before she discovered the hot blood and the passion she'd also been hiding from herself.

In the meantime he was going to be spending some long, uncomfortable nights in an empty bed. Swearing softly, Gray padded barefoot across the room to the decanter of sherry that had been left on an end table by an attentive member of the hotel staff. Sherry wasn't his favorite nightcap, but he couldn't be choosy tonight. He poured himself an ounce and walked back to the window with the glass in his hand. He switched off the lamp and stood staring broodingly out into the darkness.

Twitchell was right. The desert could be a lonely place.

AMBER AWOKE THE NEXT MORNING with her temper firmly under control. She was still rather appalled that she had reacted so strongly to the situation in which she found herself, but in the bright morning sunlight she found plenty of excuses for her odd burst of emotion.

She'd been under a certain amount of stress after all. Any wedding was a stressful event. And she'd apparently been under a misapprehension, too. She'd assumed Gray had intended the relationship between himself and his new bride to be a reasonably normal one.

She dressed in jeans and a pastel shirt and walked out into the sitting room of the suite to discover that Gray had already left for his business meeting. There was a note on the table in his large, scrawling handwriting that said he would meet her for lunch in the hotel lobby. He suggested she go swimming after breakfast.

There was, naturally, no mention of the small scene in his bedroom the previous evening. Amber wrinkled her nose as she crumpled the note and tossed it in the small, discreet trash container.

Her main reaction to last night's unfortunate confrontation was one of embarrassment. It wasn't like her to lose her temper. It also wasn't like Gray to lose his. They had both been under an unusual amount of tension, Amber decided, and neither had quite realized it. She would devote herself today to restoring the easy harmony that had characterized their relationship for nearly three months. Amber had a hunch that Gray would do the same.

They really were much alike in many ways, she thought complacently as she went downstairs to have breakfast in the cheerful hotel coffee shop. The unpleasant scene last night would be ignored by both of them in the light of a new day. Neither would refer to it again and matters between them would resume their normal, comfortable tenor. They would both pretend nothing had happened, Amber thought with a sense of relief.

She was absolutely right. Gray met her for lunch, his gaze welcoming and warm. Amber joined him with a smile as he took her hand and guided her into the dining room.

"How did the meeting with the bookkeeping staff go this morning?" she asked pleasantly after they had given their orders to the waitress.

"Smooth as silk."

Amber's eyebrows lifted. "Do I sense a hidden meaning there?"

Gray buttered a slice of French bread. "You do. Things went almost too well this morning. The records are in excellent shape. Very clear, very healthy looking. They're in such good shape, in fact, that I've decided to take the afternoon off and play golf. Care to join me?"

She grinned. "I'm a lousy player."

"So am I. But it seems a shame not to take advantage of all the amenities, doesn't it?"

"You've got something up your sleeve, Gray. What is it?"

"I'll tell you on the eleventh green."

"Aha. Mystery upon mystery. What's so special about the eleventh green?"

He bit off a large chunk of the French bread with his strong teeth and chewed reflectively. "I think I'd rather talk about it on the course."

"Afraid the dining room is bugged?" Amber teased.

"You know me. I don't take chances."

"Yes," Amber agreed, feeling content. "I know you." She was sure she did. Last night's confrontation had been an aberration on both their parts.

They rented two sets of golf clubs later that afternoon and set out to play the sophisticated, challenging course. The lush grass of the fairways and putting greens created an inviting contrast to the desert foothills that cradled the golf course.

"It's like an oasis in the middle of the desert, isn't it?" Amber said as she prepared to tee off on the first hole. It had been quite a while since she had last played, and she knew her swing was going to be painfully rusty.

Gray stayed silent until she had hit the ball. The drive wasn't very long, but at least it had been fairly straight down the center of the fairway. Amber was grateful for small favors. She stepped back and inserted her club into the bag on the back of the motorized golf cart she and Gray were using.

"Not bad," Gray observed kindly.

"I hope you're as bad as you say you are," Amber told him. "If you're not, you're going to get awfully bored waiting for me on each fairway."

"Wait and see," he told her dryly.

Amber smiled as she watched him swing the club with smooth, easy power. It didn't surprise her at all when the small white ball sailed straight down the fairway in a long, gliding arc that took it far past her own shot.

"I knew it," she said as she climbed into the cart beside him. "You're very good at this. When you start getting impatient with my shots, remember it was your suggestion we play golf."

"I'll remember. And don't worry about me getting impatient. I happen to detest golf."

She glanced at him in surprise. "Then why are we playing?"

"Because I want to take a close look at the eleventh green."

"Too bad we have to play ten more holes of golf before we get to the eleventh green," Amber murmured.

"Unfortunately, I couldn't think of any other way of taking a look at it without arousing suspicion."

"Going to tell me what's going on now that we're safely away from the hotel?" Amber waited expectantly. Gray was usually quite forthcoming about his business affairs. He treated her as an equal and had always seemed to welcome her input.

"According to the records I looked at this morning, management spent a lot of money restoring the eleventh green and most of the fairway after it was washed out by a flash flood last winter," Gray said slowly as he steered the small, shaded cart along the narrow path.

"So?"

"A *lot* of money, Amber. I happened to talk to one of the groundskeepers this morning. He casually mentioned that flash floods in the foothills had been anticipated when the hotel was built. The golf course was well protected by certain construction techniques that are supposed to channel water around it. Still, nature is unpredictable. Accidents can happen."

"The plot thickens. Tell me what you suspect, Gray."

"That same groundskeeper was working here last winter. He remembers when the flood occurred and what damage was done to the hotel grounds." Gray stopped the cart on the path near the point where Amber's ball had landed. "He said the golf course had come through several storms unscathed."

"Uh-oh. I think I'm getting the point." Amber eyed the vast distance that still remained between her golf ball and the putting green that marked the end of the first hole. She selected an iron and walked out onto the fairway. Her second shot veered raggedly to the left, and she held her breath hoping it wouldn't land in the rough.

"You're safe," Gray called cheerfully.

Amber shielded her eyes with her hand, trying to see where the ball had landed. "I can't even see it."

"Don't worry, I've got it marked."

She climbed back into the cart. "Okay, Sherlock Holmes, tell me the rest of the tale and your deductions."

"Quite simple, my dear Watson. I strongly suspect Vic Delaney took advantage of the flooding last year to claim far more damage than actually occurred. He wrote off thousands of dollars as repairs to the eleventh green."

"Hmmm."

Gray nodded. "Exactly what I said. Hmmm."

"Still, that doesn't mean much other than the fact that Delaney isn't above cheating on his taxes or his insurance claims. It doesn't imply the hotel itself is in financial difficulties," Amber pointed out logically.

"No, but finding that sort of thing right at the start of an investigation makes me curious."

"I know." Amber had seen him at work before. Gray's particular brand of curiosity and the tenacious way he went about satisfying it was what made him such a valuable and expensive consultant to people like Symington. "Well, we'll just have to keep slogging along until we get to the eleventh hole."

"Correction. We'll have to keep slogging along until we finish all eighteen. It would be a little obvious if we turned around at the eleventh green and headed back to the pro shop, wouldn't it?"

"I'm going to be exhausted," Amber warned. "It's getting very warm out here."

"Puts me in mind of another Twitchell poem," Gray mused. "'Ambush Under a Scorching Sun.'"

"I remember that one," Amber said brightly. "It was another one in which Twitchell made a lot of references to hot lead and burning iron. You know, until Ms Abercrombie wrote that letter to you, I hadn't realized just how much of Twitchell's work teems with veiled sexual innuendoes."

"You didn't realize it because his poems aren't teeming with veiled sexual innuendoes," Gray stated firmly. "And in my letter to Ms Abercrombie I shall spell that out for her in great detail. I shall spell it out in even greater detail in my next article for *Poets of the Southwest*."

"I'm sure she'll be thrilled to hear from the world's only other Twitchell scholar," Amber said with grave amusement.

"I am not the world's only *other* Twitchell expert," Gray retorted grandly. "I am the world's *only* Twitchell expert."

"Ms Abercrombie might take issue with you."

"Ms Abercrombie is a fake and a fraud and I intend to prove it."

"After you prove to yourself that the eleventh green wasn't recently repaired to the tune of several thousand dollars?" Amber suggested.

"Exactly. Everything in good time. Justice shall prevail, just as it always does in Twitchell's ballads."

The eleventh green looked like all the other greens to Amber's admittedly inexperienced eye. Gray walked around it and spent some time in the rough grass beyond the smooth, velvety green. He wasn't searching for a lost ball, Amber knew. She finally putted her way into the cup after three embarrassing tries and then held the flag for Gray, who sank his ball in one negligent putt.

"I sure am glad you don't love golf," she muttered as she replaced the flag.

"It's a stupid, boring game." He tossed his putter into the golf bag and got behind the wheel of the cart.

"If you find it stupid and boring, how did you find time to get so good at it?"

"I'm not really good at it. I learned to play well enough not to embarrass myself in front of clients. That's all. A lot of them play golf, unfortunately."

Amber eyed him skeptically. She had a hunch he hadn't had much trouble becoming proficient at the sport. With his natural strength and smooth, masculine grace, he probably hadn't ever had much trouble with anything that required coordination and power.

That thought brought back memories of the previous night when she had lain awake for quite some time wondering what it would have been like to lie in Gray's arms. Sternly Amber pushed the disturbing images aside. Things were back to normal between herself and Gray. She was determined to keep them that way.

"What's on the agenda for this evening?" she asked.

"Tonight we're going to ask for a bottle of very exotic French wine at dinner."

"We are? I have no objections, but why French wine?"

Gray tossed her a gleaming look. "Because I don't think Delaney has this particular label in the hotel cellars. It's not on the wine list."

"Then why are we going to ask for it?"

"Because Vic Delaney spent a vast sum of money on a shipment of it. I don't think that shipment ever materialized. When we try ordering it tonight, we'll know for sure, won't we?"

"I see," Amber said quietly. She tried to sound politely businesslike, because business was clearly the only thing on Gray's mind. But privately she was beginning to understand that the second night of her honeymoon was probably going to be spent in the same way as the first had been spent—alone in her bedroom.

# 4

FOUR DAYS LATER Amber found herself experiencing S. U. Twitchell country in the most authentic way—from the back of a horse. She didn't know whether to groan or laugh as she obediently followed Gray as he led the way into a small canyon hidden in the hills behind the resort. He was astride a big sorrel gelding and seemed to be having no more difficulty adjusting to a horse's saddle than to swinging a golf club. His big frame moved easily with that of the animal's, and the sorrel seemed ready and willing to take direction from the firm hands that held the reins.

Amber's own mount was a small mare of a indeterminate pale shade that was probably meant to be palomino. It would have required more imagination than Amber had to see any resemblance between her horse and Trigger, however. She had a hunch her animal had been bleached somewhere along the line. Furthermore, Goldie, as the mare was called, refused to pay any attention to Amber's guidance. Goldie had apparently learned early on in her career as a dude ranch horse that she was only required to follow the horse in front of her. She did that much and no more.

"Are you sure this is the way Twitchell got his inspiration?" Amber demanded as Goldie plodded dutifully behind the big sorrel. They were following the path of a small creek that ran through the canyon.

"Of course, I'm sure. How else could he have developed such a feel for the land?" Gray glanced over his shoulder. His expression was respectfully sincere, but there was amusement in his green-gold eyes.

"Somehow I've never thought of Twitchell as having a great feel for the land," Amber muttered. "Or poetry, either," she added in an even lower tone.

But Gray caught the treasonous words. "You'd better smile when you say that, pardner."

"I can't smile. The part of me that meets the saddle has grown numb. When do we stop for lunch?"

Gray reined in his horse and gazed around the scenic little canyon. He seemed satisfied with the sparkling creek, the artfully designed clutter of small boulders and the welcoming bits of green foliage. "How about right here? This looks like the canyon Twitchell described in 'Outlaw Retreat,' doesn't it? Do you suppose he actually wandered into this very canyon and got inspired?"

"Any inspiration S.U.T. received probably came from the bottom of a bottle." Predictably enough Goldie had come to a halt the instant her leader had stopped. Amber swung one jeaned leg over the saddle and dropped to the ground with a feeling of relief. Goldie immediately took the action as an indication that she was free to munch. The mare started nosing around a patch of green that grew near the little creek.

"There are times when I detect a certain lack of respect for the great man in some of your comments." Gray dismounted as if he was accustomed to spending days in a saddle. He looped the sorrel's reins and those of the washed-out palomino around a scraggly bush. Then he removed a small leather pouch from the back of his saddle.

Amber grinned at him as he lounged comfortably on a rock and began to investigate the contents of the pouch. "Any lack of respect you detect is merely my poor sense of humor at work. What have you got in the pouch?"

"Some watercress-and-pâté sandwiches, a couple of packages of potato chips, some carrots and olives and two apples." He spread the small repast out on a napkin that had also been in the pouch. "And last, but not least, a split of a good, sturdy, California red."

"Not bad. The resort kitchen is very accommodating." Amber reached for one of the sandwiches.

"More accommodating than Roger and Ozzie. I thought I'd never get rid of one or the other of them this morning," Gray said as he leaned back against a sun-warmed boulder and devoured half a sandwich in one bite. Gray's appetite was in proportion to the rest of him.

"They were certainly determined to escort us on this little jaunt, weren't they?" Amber agreed thoughtfully. Gray had put his large foot down very forcefully this morning when the two young men had offered to act as guides. It had been more than a polite offer; Roger and Ozzie had been quite insistent. But Gray, in his own quiet way, could be quite stubborn. The two young men had been left behind at the resort.

"They're getting worse. Seems like I can't go anywhere on the resort without one of them following me around. It's getting to be impossible to have any discreet conversations with groundskeepers, wine stewards or housekeepers." Gray swallowed the rest of the sandwich and opened the half bottle of red wine. "I think they're beginning to realize I'm not turning into a one-man cheerleading squad for the resort."

Amber frowned. "You haven't told them you're getting suspicious of the books, have you?"

Gray raised one heavy brow, his glance sardonic. "Do I look stupid?"

"Nope."

He nodded, gratified. "Thank you. No, I haven't said anything. But I've had to ask some questions, and I'm sure the people I've talked to have reported back to Delaney. He's probably getting nervous. From what I can tell, he can't afford not to have this deal go through. He's in money trouble up to his white patent leather belt buckle."

"What's our schedule?" Amber opened a packet of olives and carrots.

"I think we'll leave the day after tomorrow, a little earlier than I'd originally planned. I'll have more than enough information by then to make a full report to Symington."

"You're going to recommend against the purchase?"

Gray bit into another sandwich. "Yeah. Not much else I can do. Symington would be an idiot to get involved in this mess."

Amber stifled a small sigh as she accepted the fact that her odd honeymoon was coming to an end. No loss, she told herself. It hadn't been much of a honeymoon, anyway. Just a working vacation of sorts. It was more depressing than she wanted to admit. She munched a carrot stick and gazed unseeingly at the horses who were nibbling sparse grass. She wondered if that was all Gray had wanted the trip to be or if he'd occasionally wanted more from his honeymoon. She couldn't get that last kiss out of her mind, but she also couldn't ignore the fact that there had been no repeat.

There was something very soothing and peaceful about the canyon. A handful of tiny birds went about their business in the bushes. The creek burbled cheerfully, and the warm sun beat down with a pleasant intensity.

"Amber?"

Surprised by the serious tone of his voice, she turned to glance at Gray. He was still leaning back against the rock, his hazel eyes studying her. A trickle of awareness went through her. Whatever he was thinking at this moment, it had nothing to do with the Symington deal. "Yes, Gray?"

"Maybe you were right the other night. Maybe we should talk."

Amber's mouth went dry. She ought to have been elated, but instinct warned her that the conversation was taking a dangerous turn. "What do you want to talk about, Gray?"

"California."

For a heartbeat or two Amber couldn't find her voice. When she did, she had a hard time keeping it even. "What about California?"

"I want to know what went wrong down there."

He knew from one or two small comments she had let slip that there had been a man in California. And Amber had a hunch her sister had dropped more than a hint or two on the brief occasions when she had met Gray. But Gray had never asked her what had happened, had never pushed past the walls of Amber's privacy. Amber had assumed he never would. His respect for her secrets was one of the many things that she'd liked about Gray; one of the things that had made her feel so comfortable in his presence. Now, for the first time, he was probing an area that she had privately labeled forbidden. Automatically she retreated, summoning up a casual smile to cover her withdrawal.

"I've always heard it's a good idea not to get involved in a big mutual confession scene with one's new husband," Amber said lightly.

"Is there a lot to confess?"

His refusal to be sidetracked by her smile annoyed Amber. Her chin lifted. "Gray, if my past was a problem for you, you should have mentioned it before you asked me to marry you."

"It's not a problem for me, but I think it is for you." His gaze was intent, faintly narrowed against the noon light. "I wasn't going to ask you about it, but recently I've started wondering if it might help to talk about it. I know there was a man. I know something went wrong and that it was bad enough to make you quit a high-paying job and head for Washington. You went north to lick your wounds and to hide, didn't you?"

"No. I went north to start over again."

"You've succeeded in doing that to a certain extent. You've got a new life, new friends, new job. But there are still a few chains binding you to the past, aren't there? You can't quite let go. Can't quite trust yourself—"

"Gray!" She cut through his words with an angry exclamation. "What's the matter with you? You've never grilled me before. I thought we had an understanding. Part of that understanding was an acceptance of each other and of the past. I certainly haven't asked you about your first marriage, have I? Damn it, you shouldn't have asked me to marry you if you had problems dealing with my background."

"I thought we could ignore whatever happened in California the same way I know we can safely ignore my first marriage. But now I'm not so sure," he said honestly.

She stared at him. "It's a little late to come to that conclusion."

His mouth curved faintly. "No, it's not. It's never too late. We've still got plenty of time."

Amber jumped to her feet, shoving her fingers into the back pocket of her jeans. She walked to the edge of the creek, turning her back to Gray. "I don't know what you want or expect from me, Gray," she said quietly. "There's no big mystery about California. I fell in love with a man and things didn't work out. That's all there is to the story, believe me. It's a depressingly common tale, and you know it."

"Are you still in love with him?"

Amber swung around, shocked. "Of course I'm not. It was all over months ago. Is that what's worrying you? You think I'm carrying the torch for him? Gray, I swear I would never have married you if that was the case." Even as she said the words aloud, Amber realized the truth behind them. Whatever else she felt for Roarke Kelley, she didn't love him.

"If you're not still carrying the torch, then you're free to fall in love with me," Gray stated softly.

Amber felt trapped and on the defensive. Frantically she began beating at the doors of an invisible cage. "I told you I wasn't in love with you when you asked me to marry you," she retorted. "At least, not in the way people usually mean when they talk of love. You said that was all right, that you weren't looking for the 'grand passion' of the century. Why are you doing this? You convinced me we could be happy together, and I believed you. I'm quite prepared to be happy with you, Gray. You're the one who's putting barricades in the way. I'm getting the feeling you've changed your mind. You want more from me than you said you did. But I don't understand why. You're no more the grand-passion type than I am. It wasn't fair of you to marry me under one set of rules and then change the rules after the wedding."

He looked up at her, hearing the emotional fervor in her words, and wanted to laugh. "You have a very passionate way of telling me you're not the passionate type. But you're right about one thing, I did change the rules on you and it wasn't fair." He dusted off his hands and collected the scraps of sandwich wrappers. "There are times when I don't play fair. Not too many, but a few."

"Gray. . ."

"Forget it." He got to his feet and held out his hand to her. There was a deep smile in his eyes. "I had no right to push you. You say you're prepared to be happy with me and that's enough for now. Come here and be happy with me, sweetheart."

Amber's wary gaze went from his face to his outstretched hand. "I'm not sure about this, Gray," she said uncertainly.

"I am. So stop worrying and come here. It's time we headed back to the ranch. Roger and Ozzie will be getting nervous."

She heard the easygoing amusement return to his voice, and Amber relaxed once more. Smiling a little tremulously, she stepped forward and put her fingers in his. Gray leaned down and kissed her lightly. "Don't look so serious. Everything's going to be fine. Wait and see. Trust me?"

Amber nodded, not knowing what else to say. On some level she did trust him, but she felt as if she no longer understood him completely. That was making her nervous, she knew. She wanted to be happy with Gray, and she longed for him to be happy and content with her. But he was beginning to make that simple goal difficult. Somehow she was going to have to tear down the barriers Gray was erecting.

AMBER DRESSED FOR DINNER that night with a grim determination that belied the festive intent of the evening ahead. Tonight was "fiesta" night at the hotel. All of the guests were invited to a gala celebration in the dining room and lounge. Management had promised a Mexican buffet, strolling mariachis, stuffed piñatas and a lively dance band in the lounge. Everyone was encouraged to dress appropriately for the occasion. The hotel clothing boutique had done a lively business that day in imported Mexican shirts, colorful, flounced skirts and off-the-shoulder peasant blouses.

As she tied the bright pink sash at the waist of her wide turquoise skirt and adjusted the low elasticized neckline of the frilly peasant blouse, Amber wondered how the resort could possibly be in any financial difficulty. Talk about a trapped clientele. The profits from the clothing boutique alone on "fiesta" days should have been enough to keep the business afloat.

But Gray had told her that there were serious discrepancies in the accounting books, and she believed him. He knew his business.

He might not know how to make love to his wife, but he definitely knew his business.

Amber made a face at herself in the mirror and pulled the neckline of the blouse a little lower. It was off her shoulders now, exposing a great deal of skin above the gentle swell of her breasts. Even her bathing suit wasn't cut that low. This, she thought disparagingly, was what came from feeling a little desperate. The sense of desperation stemmed from having spent the preceding three nights in a bed by herself.

So she wasn't a sex kitten. Maybe she didn't have the flamboyant interest in sex that some other women had. What did it matter if she was the quiet, even-tempered type? That didn't mean she didn't have any interest at all in having her husband make love to her. This business of sleeping apart was getting on her nerves. It wasn't normal or natural, and she didn't understand why Gray was insisting on it. Husbands and wives, even the less passionate types, were supposed to sleep together. Surely it was part of being happy and content together.

If Gray was really waiting for her to come on to him like a lusty, impassioned little nymphomaniac, he would wait forever. Amber wasn't about to get that carried away by her own emotions or desires. But perhaps she could give her husband a few more overt hints tonight. Surely with a few gentle pushes he would realize that they could be quite happy and satisfied with each other in bed as well as out of it. And perhaps if he were content with her in that department, he would stop pushing for answers about her past, answers Amber didn't have.

Amber didn't fully understand why Gray was holding out for some sign of overwhelming passion from her in the first place. He hadn't seemed to want it when he'd asked her to marry him. She'd never had any indication that he was the type to demand a sizzling, tempestuous female in his bed. He'd seemed quite content with the bargain he had made with her. Perhaps it was the emergence of some aspect of latent male ego, Amber thought ruefully. Whatever it was, she intended to try to overcome his scruples and doubts tonight. The relationship between them during the day was as normal and smooth-running as it had always been, if one discounted that small scene in the canyon this afternoon. There was no reason the nights shouldn't also become normal and smooth-running.

Amber stepped away from the mirror with a flounce of her brightly colored skirts. She had decided to wear her hair down for the evening. It danced around her bare shoulders in a bouncy sweep of golden-brown curls. She picked up the oversized Mexican straw purse she had bought to go with her vividly colored new clothes and swung it over her arm. Then she opened her bedroom door.

Gray was seated in a wicker chair reading a newspaper. He'd reluctantly consented to buy an embroidered open-throated white shirt that had been made in Acapulco. It was his sole contribution toward the evening's festivities. With it he wore slacks. His dark hair was combed into its usual severe style. It was still damp from the shower. He looked up as Amber came into the room. She smiled and did a small pirouette.

"How do I look?" she asked.

"As though you're about to fall out of that blouse," he retorted, looking both surprised and disapproving.

"Nonsense. All the other women are going to be wearing blouses just like it tonight. They were selling like hotcakes in the dress shop this afternoon. Ready to go?"

"Not quite." Deliberately he got to his feet and walked across the room to stand in front of her. He was still frowning at the low neckline of the blouse. "Can't you pull it up a bit higher?"

"Why should I?" she asked innocently. "It was made to be worn this way. It's not any worse than a swimsuit, Gray."

"It's a lot worse than *your* swimsuit." He put his hand on her bare shoulder and slid his fingers just under the elasticized edge of the blouse.

Amber was so startled at the unexpectedly intimate touch that she nearly stumbled when she automatically stepped backward. Her eyes met Gray's in a moment of shared communication that sent a wave of warmth through her whole body. She went very still as, without taking his eyes from hers, he gently eased the neckline of the blouse up to a higher level. When he was finished, Gray glanced down at the results of his handiwork.

"Much better," he said blandly.

"I think, Cormick Grayson, that deep down inside, you may be a little straitlaced. Old-fashioned perhaps. Possibly even prudish." Her skin still burned from the light touch of his fingers. It was all Amber could do to make her comment sound teasing.

"The word you're looking for is possessive, Mrs. Grayson. Keep it in mind. Are you ready to go?"

His response was sardonic and tinged with humor, but there was something in his eyes that was totally serious. Amber wasn't sure how to interpret the expression. She inched the strap of her straw bag higher on her bare shoulder. "I'm ready. Let's go eat tacos until we can't see straight."

"A sentiment of which S.U.T. would undoubtedly approve."

"Did he ever do an ode to tacos?" Amber asked brightly as they left the room and headed toward the elevators.

"No. but I believe there is a mention or two of tequila somewhere in the body of his work."

"I'll bet. There was probably a fair amount of tequila within Twitchell's own body when he was writing some of his more memorable pieces," Amber declared. "Actually, tequila sounds like a good idea at the moment. I need something to numb the aftereffects of that ride into the canyon."

"I thought you were already numb from it," Gray said with a chuckle as they stepped into the elevator.

"Unfortunately, the numbing effect has worn off. It's been replaced by some very vivid memories of life in the saddle."

"A little sore?"

"That's putting it mildly. Thank heavens the seats in the dining room are well cushioned," Amber said in heartfelt tones.

Dinner was a lively event, as promised by Vic Delaney. The mariachi band strolled through the dining room singing Mexican love songs while the guests helped themselves from a huge buffet that included everything from tamales to flan. There was a wide assortment of creative interpretations of Mexican cooking in between the two traditional favorites. Mexican beer, margaritas and tequila with salt and lime were available in abundance. The drinks were on the house tonight, and the guests weren't hesitating to indulge themselves.

"Are you sure the resort is in financial trouble?" Amber asked dubiously. She was working her way through the buffet line. Gray was right behind her. "How could Delaney afford this kind of spread if he's hurting?"

"Window dressing. You have to keep up appearances when you're trying to sell something as expensive as this place."

"I suppose so. Still, this is such elaborate window dressing."

"The bigger the deal, the more elaborate it has to be."

"Is Symington going to be disappointed?"

"Symington is a businessman. He's not emotionally involved with the deal. Now hush. I don't want either member of the dynamic duo overhearing you."

Amber glanced around and saw Roger standing a few feet away. He was assisting guests with free beer. Ozzie was on the other side of the room entertaining two elderly women. "Those two do get around, don't they?"

"They're Delaney's men."

Vic Delaney himself was playing the genial host this evening, ensuring that all his guests were having a good time. He strolled toward Amber and Gray as they headed for one of the large communal tables that had been set up for dining. It was a night when guests were supposed to socialize, and that meant sharing a dinner table with other guests.

"How are you two doing?" Delaney asked jovially. He slapped Gray familiarly on the back. "Did you try some of the shrimp? It's a specialty of my chef's. We fly the shrimp in fresh from the coast just for him. He won't touch the frozen stuff. A real prima donna. But I guess every good chef is. What did you folks do today? Ozzie said you took a couple of horses and headed for the hills."

"My wife wanted to see some of the countryside," Gray murmured politely as he settled Amber into a seat next to a white-haired gentleman. "I'm afraid we may have overdone it. Amber isn't used to sitting in a saddle for a couple of hours."

Delaney gave Amber a rueful grin. "Sorry about that. Try a nice warm soak in the tub tonight. Does wonders." He nodded around the table, smiling at the other guests. "Have a good time tonight. Remember, the drinks are on the house."

There was a general murmur of appreciation from the circle at the table, and Delaney sauntered on to the next group of diners. The silver-haired man sitting next to Amber smiled beneath his trim mustache. "Personally, I'm sticking to the golf course while I'm here. I haven't been in a saddle in years. I can just imagine the effects!"

His wife laughed and introduced herself. The two other couples at the table did, too, and soon the conversation drifted into the casual, meaningless chatter required among strangers forced to share a meal. Everyone was quite good-natured about the seating arrangements, however, and appeared willing to be caught up in the fiesta mood. The endless flow of beer and tequila-based drinks helped.

Halfway through dinner the young woman sitting across from Amber said something about Western folklore, and Amber seized the opportunity.

"Funny you should mention Arizona legends," she said cheerfully. "My husband is something of an expert in the field of Western poetry."

Immediately all heads turned toward Gray, who shot Amber a chiding glance.

"I don't believe I'm familiar with any Western poets," someone said thoughtfully.

"Gray's field of expertise is Sherborne Ulysses Twitchell," Amber confided.

"Really?" The young woman looked interested. "When did he live?"

"His birth date is a little uncertain," Amber said. "When Gray does his articles about Twitchell, he usually writes 'born ?' in the biographical notes."

"When did he die?" the white-haired gentleman sitting next to Amber inquired politely.

"Gray usually puts 'died ?' in that section of the notes."

Gray jumped into the conversation before Amber could cause it to deteriorate further. "That's a bit misleading," he assured the other guests smoothly. "We're almost positive Twitchell died sometime in 1901."

"What happened to him?" someone asked.

Gray cleared his throat. "There appears to have been an accident in a hotel in which he was staying. He was traveling toward Mexico, from what I've been able to determine, and had stopped for the night in a little town just this side of the border. Apparently there was a fight."

"A gunfight?" the young woman demanded, looking quite interested now.

"So it appears. Shots were exchanged in one of the hotel rooms that night according to a newspaper story the next day. One unidentified body was buried. There is no mention of Twitchell after that incident, but his name was definitely on the hotel register according to the newspaper accounts. Since he published no poetry after that date, I think it's safe to assume it was his body that was buried."

"Why wasn't he identified?"

Amber grinned. "Because the body was naked when it was found. Except for a pair of socks, that is."

"How odd," the gentleman next to Amber observed.

"Not really. From what Gray discovered in the newspaper article, Twitchell was in bed at the time of the shooting."

"Murdered?"

"Depends on your point of view," Amber informed them all with great relish. "S.U.T. was in bed with a *woman* when he was killed."

"Now, Amber, you're getting into an area of sheer conjecture," Gray warned loftily as he reached for his tequila.

Amber grinned. "The hotel, you see, was actually a bordello. Twitchell made the mistake of climbing into bed with a lady who happened to be the favorite of one of the other patrons. The patron took exception to the situation."

"How extraordinary," the white-haired gentleman marveled. "Got himself killed in a fight over a lady of the night."

"I don't think it could have been much of a fight," Amber said blithely. "From what Gray discovered in the newspaper account, Twitchell never even got a chance to draw his gun."

"Well, it sounds as though he probably died happy," the older man remarked with a satisfied nod.

There was a moment of silence around the table and then everyone burst out laughing. The conversation after that loosened up a great deal. Amber threw Gray a teasing glance, and he returned the look with a faint gleam in his eyes.

"You're not doing much for S.U.T.'s reputation as a respectable poet," Gray complained.

"He hasn't got a reputation as a respectable poet. I've decided he might as well have one as an unrespectable poet."

When dinner was over, many of the guests drifted into the large, dimly lit lounge for the floor show. Dancing was to follow, and Amber settled back to enjoy the evening. Surreptitiously she used the concealing shadows to tug down the elasticized neckline of the peasant blouse. Gray appeared unaware of her movements. His attention was on Roger, who was standing near the door, discreetly supervising the lounge staff. Ozzie was nowhere in sight.

Amber leaned over to say something to Gray, but she was interrupted by the flourish of trumpets that opened the lounge act. After that there was no opportunity to carry on a conversation. The comedian was surprisingly funny, and the singer was quite good. The magician was the best part. Amber had one or two thoughts about what the whole production must have cost, but by now she expected the best from Delaney.

When the show was over, the dance band swung into action. Amber was waiting for Gray to ask her to dance when Delaney materialized beside the small table.

"Mind if I steal your wife for a few minutes?" Delaney asked Gray. "I've been looking for an opportunity to dance with her for three nights."

Amber waited for Gray to politely decline the request. She was so startled when he nodded his head that she couldn't think of any excuse to refuse. She shot her husband an irritated glance as she obediently allowed Vic Delaney to lead her out onto the floor. Gray didn't appear to notice her annoyance. He was still casually watching Roger. Determinedly Amber turned on her high-voltage client smile for her dancing partner.

"I hope you and your husband have enjoyed your stay here at the resort, Mrs. Grayson," Delaney said easily as he swung Amber into a polished series of steps. He had obviously had a lot of practice dancing with hotel guests.

"Very much," Amber replied, feeling like a fraud. It was difficult to keep up the effusive guest act when you knew your host was in deep financial water and that your husband was about to let him drown. There were aspects of Gray's business that bordered on the ruthless. Of course, she reminded herself, none of Delaney's problems were Gray's fault. Gray was just the hired gun who had been paid to investigate the situation. He owed his loyalty to his client, not Vic Delaney. "You've built quite a place here, Mr. Delaney. Very impressive."

"Call me Vic," he said with a charming smile. He whirled her around, steering her to the far side of the floor. The crowd of dancers cut them off from sight of the table where Gray was sitting. "Have you and your husband been married long?"

"Not long." She couldn't bring herself to admit she was supposed to be on her honeymoon. She still didn't know if it was Gray who had ordered the two-bedroom suite. If he had, it would seem a little odd to Delaney to learn that his guests were honeymooners. By no stretch of the imagination was she having a real wedding trip. Deliberately Amber tried to turn the conversation again. "How long have you owned your resort, Vic?"

"A while."

He was almost a vague as she was, Amber thought ruefully. "The desert makes a wonderful change from the Northwest," she plowed on brightly. "I'm actually getting accustomed to all the sunlight."

Delaney laughed politely and followed her conversational lead. When the dance ended he asked her for another one. With a trace of unease Amber gently declined. He accepted the refusal with a cheerful smile and guided her back to the table. Amber frowned as she made her way through the romantic gloom of the room.

The table where she had left Gray sitting alone with his tequila was empty.

"Looks like your husband stepped out for a minute," Delaney observed. "Since he's not available, will you reconsider the second dance?"

Amber shook her head and sat down with a self-deprecating chuckle. "I don't think so, thank you, Vic. That horseback ride really did stiffen up a few muscles today. If you don't mind, I think I'd rather watch the dancing for the rest of this evening."

"I understand completely. Let me know if you change your mind."

"Thanks." She smiled politely and watched him disappear into the crowd. A moment later he was back out on the floor with another of his guests.

A few minutes later Amber drummed her nails on the table and glanced at her watch. How long did a man normally spend in the men's room?

Assuming Gray had gone to the men's room.

Amber glanced thoughtfully toward the door of the lounge, noticing that neither Roger nor Ozzie were in sight. That was odd. Usually one or both were in the vicinity.

A few more minutes passed with no sign of Gray. His half-finished glass of tequila sat on the table in front of Amber. The more she looked at it, the more uneasy she became. It wasn't like Gray to simply disappear without an explanation.

Feeling oddly concerned, Amber got to her feet, picked up her huge straw shoulder bag and slipped out of the lounge. The spacious lobby was nearly empty.

Driven by a strange premonition that had no logic behind it, Amber pushed through the sliding glass doors that opened onto the pool terrace.

She emerged into the balmy darkness just in time to see three figures disappear around the corner at the far end of the wide, meandering gardens. The man in the center of the trio was identifiable not only by his size and build but by the way he moved. It was Gray, and he was being escorted away from the lights of the resort by Roger and Ozzie. Even as Amber watched, the three men vanished into the night-shrouded desert foothills.

# 5

AMBER'S FINGERS TIGHTENED around the strap of her straw bag as she watched the three men walk out of sight. She was more than uneasy now. She was frightened. It didn't require any feminine intuition or brilliant deductive reasoning to realize there was something very wrong about the whole scenario. It was as simple as one, two, three.

One: Cormick Grayson prepares to turn in a negative financial report on Vic Delaney's resort. Two: Vic Delaney conveniently asks Grayson's wife to dance for the first time in four evenings. Three: Grayson disappears in the company of two well-muscled young men while unsuspecting wife is otherwise occupied on the dance floor.

It could, of course, all be very innocent, Amber told herself as she began making her way through the shadowed terrace gardens. But Gray had said nothing about any business meetings this evening. Surely he would have mentioned an appointment. It certainly wasn't like him to simply vanish while she was dancing with another man.

Then again, she thought as she skirted the silent, underwater-lit pool, she wasn't really sure how Gray felt about her dancing with another man. She'd never danced with anyone else in front of him. He had certainly let her go into Delaney's arms without any protest.

She was well beyond the brightly lit lobby now. On this side of the hotel the foothills rose immediately at the border of the terraced grounds. The gardens ended and the natural terrain took over shortly beyond the children's playing area. The discreet garden lights faded quickly after that. But, just as in a typical Twitchell poem, the sky was filled with stars, and there was even a sliver of a moon to light Amber's path.

The trouble was that she wasn't certain where she was going. She had lost sight of the three men just as she'd stepped out of the lobby. She had been walking in the same general direction in which they had disappeared, but she was no longer sure she was on the right path now. When her sandaled feet stepped off green lawn and landed on desert sand, she came to a halt and tried to listen. Around her the ground was twisted and convoluted as it began the process of changing from foothills into a mountain. A giant saguaro loomed up in her path, ghostly and overbearing. There was a brief scuttling sound somewhere in the vicinity of Amber's feet. The knowledge that the desert was not, by any stretch of the imagination, an empty, barren place hit her with full impact. She didn't want to think about what else was running around out here besides herself. Unfortunately there was no sign of anything two-footed.

She was about to turn to the right and search in that direction when voices drifted toward her, carried quite clearly on the still desert air. Amber froze, listening intently.

"You gotta understand how badly Mr. Delaney wants this deal to go through, Mr. Grayson," Roger was saying quite earnestly. "I'm afraid he's been getting the impression you aren't planning to recommend the sale to your client. Mr. Delaney is getting kind of worried."

"My business is with Delaney, not with you, Roger." Gray's voice sounded calm, even slightly bored. "I don't appreciate your boss sending you and your friend to make me see the error of my ways."

"You got it all wrong." This was Ozzie, sounding deeply concerned about any false impressions that might have been given to a guest. "Mr. Delaney just wants us to put a proposition to you."

"Why didn't he put this proposition to me himself? No offense, gentlemen, but I see you two more in the role of brawn than brain."

"Mr. Delaney's busy tonight."

"Sure. You mean he preferred not to get his hands dirty in the event something goes wrong." Gray sounded amused. "Very wise of him."

Roger spoke up again, his voice tightening a little. "This proposition of Mr. Delaney's could make you a rich man, Grayson. For your own sake, you'd better listen."

"He's offering a bribe for me to doctor the report going to my client? No wonder he didn't want to come along with you two. He's going to deny any connection to this if it turns sour, isn't he? He'll claim you were acting on your own. Just a couple of overly enthusiastic, loyal employees. Doesn't that make you guys a little nervous?"

Amber took a deep breath and managed to unstick her sandaled feet. She took a tentative step toward the small rise that shielded the three men. There had been no threat of violence, but her heart was pounding. Something was very wrong here. Gray would never take a bribe. She was utterly sure of that. Unfortunately she wasn't at all sure of what Roger and Ozzie would do if he refused. Roger and Ozzie seemed quite devoted to Vic Delaney.

The conversation continued as Amber edged her way closer, but she only caught bits and pieces of it. The voices carried well on the night air, but so did the sounds of the dance band playing in the lounge behind her. Occasionally the music overwhelmed the more delicate thread of the quiet conversation taking place behind the hillock.

"... thousand dollars sound, Mr. Grayson?" Roger asked with cool satisfaction as Amber halted behind the shelter of another ancient saguaro.

"It sounds like it's meant to sound," Gray murmured. "Like a great deal of money. I'm afraid I'll have to refuse, however. I'm sure you can understand my position. It's bad for business if word gets out that I can be bought this easily."

"No one has to know," Ozzie said, sounding more earnest than ever.

"I'll know. You'll know. Your friend here will know, and so will Delaney. That's not exactly a small crowd. Now, if you'll excuse me, I should be getting back to my wife. She'll be wondering where I am."

"Don't you worry about your wife," Roger said. "Mr. Delaney's taking good care of her."

"Is he?" For the first time there was a distinct edge in Gray's voice. Until now he had sounded half bored and wryly disgusted. But things had changed. The two younger men must have sensed it because they suddenly became a little harder sounding and a little less anxious to please.

"You don't seem to understand just how much Mr. Delaney wants you to take this commission he's offer-

ing, Grayson. If you've got any sense, you'll stop acting heroic and start acting sensible. He'll give you the
money in cash just as soon as the deal closes."

"Forget it."

There was a rustle of movement, and Amber realized that Roger and Ozzie had probably moved forward to cut off Gray's exit.

"Sorry about this, Grayson, but we can't let you go
back until we've made you see how important this deal
is to our boss." Ozzie didn't sound at all sorry. There
was an undercurrent of anticipation in his words, as if
this were the moment in the confrontation he, personally, had been looking forward to with some enthusiasm.

Amber waited no longer. She put her hand inside the
big straw purse and stepped around the small mound
of brush and sand. "Excuse me, gentlemen, but I've
come to claim my husband."

All three men turned to stare at her in astonishment.
Amber shivered as she took in the way Roger and Ozzie were obviously about to close in on Gray. Gray was
standing with his feet slightly apart, his hands held
easily at his sides. He seemed even more startled than
Roger and Ozzie to see her.

"Amber..." Gray began. He cut off his own words
as she smiled quite brilliantly and moved the purse a
few meaningful inches. Her right hand was still buried
inside the straw bag.

"Hello, Gray. I had a hunch you'd gone out for a
stroll. You should have said something. You know how
I always insist on being present at your little im-
promptu business meetings." She directed her smile at
Roger and Ozzie, who were glowering at her. In the

starlight she could see their faces quite clearly. Roger responded first to the intrusion.

"Get out of here, Mrs. Grayson. We've got a few things to discuss with your husband." His words were rough but his attention was on her purse. Ozzie's frowning gaze was also on the bag.

"I'm afraid I can't leave Gray out here all alone," Amber explained politely. "You see, he pays me good money to stick around on these business trips just in case folks such as yourselves get carried away with en- thusiasm for the deal." Amber paused and added de- liberately, "I'm not exactly Gray's wife. Why do you think he requested a suite with two bedrooms, gentle- men? My job is to keep an eye on him, but it's strictly business."

There was a moment of stunned silence. All eyes were fastened on the straw purse. Amber hoped Roger and Ozzie were busy visualizing the gun they apparently thought she was holding inside. With any luck they'd have seen enough television during their formative years to make the image very clear. Gray, at least, wasn't going to give the game away. She knew that af- ter one quick glance at his impassive face.

Ozzie finally looked intently at Amber as she stood facing them. "Who are you? Grayson's bodyguard?"

"Mr. Grayson prefers to call me his personal assis- tant." Amber paused for effect. "And sometimes he calls me his wife." She didn't glance at her husband as she asked calmly, "Ready to go, Gray?"

"I'm ready." His teeth flashed briefly in the shadows as he strolled forward to stand beside her. The small grin was both amused and a little dangerous. "Remind me to thank you later for rescuing me from a very bor- ing meeting."

"My pleasure." Amber was aware of a flood of excitement that was blotting out her fear. It was going to work. Roger and Ozzie believed her at least enough to be wary of her. They were almost convinced she was Gray's bodyguard. "I think we should be getting back to the hotel now."

"There's just one more thing," Gray murmured. He smiled at Roger. "I'd like the keys to the Jeep you keep parked in front of the lobby, please."

"What the hell are you taking about?"

Gray held out his hand. "Amber and I have had enough Southwestern hospitality for one year. We're leaving town tonight and we'll need transportation to the airport. I don't think I want to impose on either you or Ozzie, so we won't ask you to drive us in the limo. Just give me the keys to the Jeep."

Roger hesitated, his expression hardening with a helpless rage. He shot a quick, assessing glance at Amber who continued to hold the straw bag at about the level of his chest. Then, obviously gritting his teeth, Roger reached into his pocket and withdrew a set of keys. "Mr. Delaney isn't going to like this."

Gray caught the keys easily as Roger flung them at him. "Mr. Delaney isn't the only one who's a little upset at the moment. I can't say I'm all that pleased with the situation myself. Definitely time to cut this trip short. Don't think it hasn't been fun. Let's go, Amber."

Amber slid him a quick glance, unsure of how to handle the retreat. She felt she ought to keep the imaginary gun trained on Roger and Ozzie, but that would mean backing up the whole distance to the hotel lobby. Gray understood her dilemma at once. He took her arm and swung her around to head back toward the resort.

"Don't worry about Roger and Ozzie, my love. I'm sure they understand the situation perfectly. They're not going to get in our way now."

She wasn't sure how he could be so certain of that, but she knew Gray well enough to respect his understanding of human nature. If he thought they were temporarily safe from the two muscle men, he was probably right. Keeping her hand inside her purse, she allowed herself to be walked briskly back toward the safety of the lobby lights. There was no sound of pursuit.

"Are we really going to leave tonight?" she asked as Gray ushered her through the wide glass doors. Inside the lobby everything looked normal and serene. It was hard to believe the scene that had just taken place out in the desert.

"We are." Gray was already leading her toward the elevators. "The sooner the better. You've got five minutes to throw everything into a suitcase."

"That's not enough time to pack!"

"I'll replace whatever you have to leave behind," he told her blandly. "I'll deduct the cost from whatever I'm paying you for your bodyguarding services."

"Don't laugh at me, Gray," she said as they stepped out of the elevator and hurried toward their suite. "It was all I could think of on the spur of the moment."

"I'm not laughing," he assured her, his teeth showing briefly in a wicked grin as he shoved the key into the lock and opened the door. "I'm impressed. You sounded very professional out there."

"I watch television the same as everyone else," she told him flippantly. As she stepped into the room, she swung around to confront him. "What was going on out there?"

"I'll tell you on the way to the airport. You've got four minutes left." He was already moving into his own room and reaching for the shirts he'd left hanging in the closet.

Amber's head filled with a thousand questions, but she put them aside as she raced into her bedroom and collected her things. She threw her clothing into her suitcase without any regard for wrinkles and slammed the case shut. Precisely four minutes later, she and Gray were heading back down toward the lobby in the elevator. Just as they stepped out on the bottom floor, Amber hesitated.

"I think I forgot my green heels."

"I told you, I'll replace them." He had a firm hand under her arm as he led her toward the well-lit lobby entrance. His attention was on Roger and Ozzie, who were lounging against the front desk. Neither moved to stop the two guests who were departing at such an unusual hour, but there was a barely controlled anger simmering in their gazes. Delaney was nowhere in sight.

Gray was still grinning faintly as he tossed the suitcases into the Jeep and swung lightly into the driver's seat beside Amber. She glared at him.

"I get the feeling you're enjoying this," she said accusingly.

"It does make a change from the normal routine of these trips." He spun the wheel and sent the small vehicle leaping down the drive toward the main road. "I'll have to take you along more often. How much do professional bodyguards get paid?"

"A great deal more than personal assistants, I'm sure. I'll be expecting a big increase next month. Listen, Gray, this is serious. I want to know what was going on back there. When I came around the corner of that little hill, I had the impression Roger and Ozzie were about to beat you to a pulp because you weren't agreeing to accept Delaney's bribe."

"Your impression probably wasn't far wrong." He didn't sound worried.

"Well, shouldn't we go to the police?"

"And tell them what? No one laid a hand on me or you. No one even overtly threatened us. Delaney would deny all knowledge of the bribe and offer to fire Roger and Ozzie for hassling guests. That would be the end of it. We don't have any proof that anything really nasty happened. It's conceivable, in fact, that Roger and Ozzie might complain that you pulled a gun on them for no reason."

"I didn't pull a gun on them!"

Gray showed a few more teeth in his smile. "Try telling them that after the cool act with the purse. I was pretty impressed myself."

A fierce exhilaration flared in Amber. "I wasn't bad, was I?" She felt quite pleased with herself now that they were safely out of the reach of Ozzie, Roger and Vic Delaney. "Tell me exactly what was happening out there in the desert."

Gray shrugged. "Delaney must have realized I was turning negative on the deal he was offering Symington and that my report would reflect it. He decided to try a bribe. He kept you occupied on the dance floor while he sent Roger and Ozzie, to, uh, talk some sense into me."

"Do you think Delaney realized Roger and Ozzie would threaten you physically?" Amber asked.

"I'm sure Delaney knows exactly how Roger and Ozzie work."

"You don't sound particularly upset about this whole mess," Amber pointed out. "Does this sort of thing happen often on your business trips?"

"I'm afraid they usually aren't this exciting." Gray flexed his hands on the wheel and cast a quick appraising glance up at the night sky. "Sort of puts you in mind of a Twitchell poem, doesn't it? Here we are fleeing for the border under a midnight sky with gunslingers on our heels."

Amber jerked around in the seat to stare at the empty highway behind the Jeep. "I don't see anyone following us."

"A figure of speech, my love. A poetic allusion, if you will. Use your imagination. Twitchell would have appreciated the scene, I think."

Amber sank back into her seat with a groan. "If you're about to quote Twitchell to me, I've got a better suggestion."

It was too late. Gray was already into the opening lines of "Midnight Ride."

"The desert night was starry bright,
But there was crimson blood on the ground.
The gunman stood with a smoking iron
And listened, listened for the telltale sound.
Pursuit would come in a moment, in a moment all hell
Would break loose.
He must ride hard for the border or
Risk the hangman's noose."

Amber lifted an admonishing finger as Gray concluded the unmemorable lines. "Another reference to iron," she pointed out, not without a measure of satisfaction.

"Is that all you can think about at a time like this?" Gray chided her. "Here we are reliving one of Twitchell's legends and you've got literary phallic symbols on the brain."

"I think Ms Abercrombie may have inspired me," Amber muttered sotto voce.

"What's that?"

"Never mind. Are we going to stay at one of the airport hotels tonight?"

"I think we will remove temptation from Roger and Ozzie's path," Gray said thoughtfully. "We'll buy a ticket to Phoenix and stay there for the night. In the morning we'll head on back to Bellevue."

Amber's eyes widened. "You don't think Roger and Ozzie would actually try to track us down again tonight, do you?"

"No, but I'd rather not take any chances."

She couldn't argue with him on that score. Amber sat back in her seat as the Jeep raced along the lonely road back toward town. She was distinctly relieved when no headlights appeared behind them until after they were safely into the city.

Gray left the Jeep in the airport parking lot, put the keys in an envelope, addressed it to the resort and dropped the packet into a mailbox. Then he escorted Amber on board the jet.

The flight to Phoenix was a short hop, and Amber was still pulsing with excitement and nervous energy when they reached their destination. She couldn't seem to settle down, she realized. Gray, on the other hand, appeared totally relaxed after the adventure. She eyed him covertly, wondering why he wasn't more upset.

After all, he was the one who had come so close to getting pummeled by Roger and Ozzie.

Always assuming, of course, that Roger and Ozzie had actually intended to use physical persuasion. Amber frowned as she walked off the airplane. Perhaps nothing would have happened, she told herself. Gray was right; it would have been awkward to go to the police. No real threats had been made, and she had interrupted the proceedings before the two young men could demonstrate how far they meant to go in their efforts to convince Gray to accept the bribe.

"Do you think Delaney's likely to send Roger and Oz after us?" she asked as Gray led her toward a cab.

"No. Delaney's too smart to move off his own turf." He deposited Amber into the cab and told the driver to take them to the nearest large hotel.

"Did you know he was the type to resort to bribery and muscle-bound assistants when you took the Symington job?"

Gray shook his head. "You never know who will become the 'type' when he gets desperate. Delaney's no fool, though. He made a try and it didn't work. He'll back off now. After all, he'll be traumatized by the thought of having to deal with my 'bodyguard.'"

"It was a pretty good act, wasn't it?" Amber said with satisfaction. The farther she got from Tucson, the more euphoric she felt. She knew already she wasn't going to be able to sleep tonight. She was far too wound up, far too excited.

"There was only one small flaw in your act," Gray informed her blandly.

Amber was offended. "What was that?"

He looked across the seat at her. "What was all that nonsense about not being my wife?" he asked softly.

Amber blinked. "Oh, that. I thought it sounded more authentic to say I wasn't your wife. How many men marry their bodyguards?"

"I have no idea," he retorted dryly.

"If you want to know the truth," Amber announced recklessly, "I don't feel like much of a wife, anyway. As far as I can tell the only thing that's changed in our relationship is my last name. You were the one who requested the two bedrooms, weren't you? We didn't just happen to get that suite by accident."

Gray sighed. "No, we didn't just happen to get it by accident. I thought it was for the best."

Amber turned to stare out the window at the lights of Phoenix in the distance. For a moment she thought Gray might say something else, but the cab turned into the drive of a large chain hotel and there was no further opportunity for conversation.

A few minutes later she watched Gray pay the cab-driver. She was still riding the wave of restless, adrenaline-induced energy as they walked into the hotel lobby. She was feeling a little nervy, a little reckless. It was then that Amber had what she chose to think of as her second major inspiration of the evening. As soon as the idea struck, she acted on it. She didn't want to give herself a chance to think.

"I'll check in for us," she announced breezily.

Gray shot her a swift glance. He was already halfway to the front desk. "Why?"

"Because I've still got all my identification and charge cards in my own name," she explained with a knowing smile. "If Delaney does decide to track us down, he won't be looking for a couple checked in under the name Langley, will he?"

"You're really getting into this, aren't you?"

"It could be I was cut out for a life of action and adventure."

"Uh-huh." Gray sounded distinctly skeptical. "Just don't get too carried away with that notion. Go ahead and check in for us if you want. I don't think Delaney's likely to look for us, but if it will make you feel any better, I don't mind."

"Good. You can reimburse me later. This is, after all, a business expense."

"I'll want itemized receipts," he warned.

"You'll get them."

He nodded. "While you're handling that, I'm going to pick up a newspaper from the newsstand. I'll be right back." He walked off.

Amber sucked in her breath and marched to the front desk. "A room with one double bed," she announced quite clearly to the attendant. "For my husband and myself."

She almost lost her nerve as the woman behind the front desk quickly assigned her a room. Amber received the keys with an artificial smile. She wasn't sure yet what explanation to make to Gray. She could try telling him the hotel was full and this was the only room available, but he could check that out. She could try telling him the truth, but he might balk. She could try jumping on him the moment they entered the room, but Amber wasn't sure that would work. He was an awfully large man.

One thing was for certain, she decided as she watched Gray saunter across the lobby with a newspaper in one hand. She wasn't going to back down tonight. It was unlikely she'd ever have this much nerve or sense of daring again. Surely saving a man from a couple of hoods gave a woman some rights, especially when that man was her husband.

Gray looked up from the headlines and saw Amber waiting for him near the elevators. She was tossing a key in one hand, and there was a determined expression in her eyes. The look was similar to the one she'd had earlier in the evening when she'd pretended she was carrying a gun in the straw purse. Instinct warned him that she'd nerved herself for a showdown.

The knowledge sent a flicker of fire through his blood. Maybe she was right to push him. He'd been a fool to play the gentleman this long. Already he could feel his body tightening in anticipation. The sensation was not unlike the tautly alert feeling he'd experienced waiting for Roger and Ozzie to make their move.

As he got closer, he could see more than just feminine determination in Amber's beautiful, expressive eyes. There was a measure of anxiety there also. Gray found that rather endearing. She was still feeling reckless and bold from her adventure earlier in the evening, but she wasn't completely sure of herself.

The emotional sizzle caused by the near brush with violence was translating itself into something else, something equally elemental and compelling. Even if he'd wanted to resist her tonight, Gray was suddenly not at all sure he could have done so. He, too, was still aware of a residual energy and a restlessness that was left over from the scene in the desert. Above all, he was deeply aware of the fact that this woman was his wife. She belonged to him, and he had yet to claim her. He'd been an idiot to wait this long.

Amber chewed a little on her lower lip as she watched Gray approach. She couldn't read his eyes, but that didn't matter. She wasn't going to quit now. When he reached her side she held up the key. "We're all set. I got a room on the seventh floor."

"Fine. We won't need a bellboy. Not for these two pieces of luggage," Gray said smoothly, holding the elevator door for her.

Amber's palm grew damp around the key. She couldn't think of anything to say as the elevator cruised upward to the seventh floor. Gray didn't seem inclined to keep the conversation going, either. When they arrived at the right floor, he walked silently out of the elevator behind her. She was suddenly vitally aware of the size and mass of him as he followed her to the door and stood waiting while she unlocked it.

At the last possible instant Amber frantically began trying to think of ways to explain the fact that the room only contained one bed. As she pushed open the door, the words began tripping out of her mouth. She was horrified by the rambling monologue, but she couldn't seem to halt it. "The hotel is almost full, Gray. I was lucky to get this room. There's only one bed, but the woman at the front desk assured me it was a huge king and there should be plenty of room for both of us. I mean, I know you're accustomed to sleeping by yourself, but this is something of an emergency, or at least it's a highly unusual situation, and since we know each other so well and everything I figured that there wouldn't be any harm in sharing such a big bed for the evening. After all, we *are* married. It's not as if we're strangers or even just business partners, is it?" She broke off to look up at him helplessly as he calmly closed the door and locked it.

"No," Gray agreed, setting down the luggage. "It's not as if we're strangers or business partners." He reached out, his big hands closing over her shoulders.

Slowly, his eyes gleaming with sensual hunger, he pulled her into his arms. "I agree with you, Amber. It's time we became lovers."

# 6

AN EXQUISITE RELIEF permeated the heady excitement that was simmering in Amber's veins. She didn't know why Gray was suddenly willing to put their relationship on a normal footing, and just at that moment she didn't particularly care. The uneasy waiting was over. Everything was going to be all right now. She could know the comfort and strength of Gray's arms, and in return she would do her best to give him the physical satisfaction a man was supposed to receive from his wife. The marriage would begin for real tonight.

"I'm so glad, Gray," she breathed as she wound her arms around his neck. "I was beginning to worry that we'd made a terrible mistake." Her eyes shone up at him as she leaned into his warmth.

"So you decided to take things into your own hands tonight, is that it?" His mouth curved slightly as he lifted his hands to her hair and slid his fingers heavily through the tousled curls. The combs came free, and he caught them and pocketed them. Then his hands returned to her hair. He seemed to be savoring the feel of it.

"Things haven't been exactly normal between us this past week, Gray," she said very seriously. "I know you're waiting for some sign of latent passion lurking in my soul, but the truth is what you see is what you get. There's no fiery temptress waiting to emerge. I need to know if you're really going to be satisfied with what I am. I warned you in the beginning that I might not be the right woman for you, but you seemed so sure of yourself."

"I am sure of myself," he told her simply. His eyes were heating from green to gold as he looked down into her anxious face. "And I think it's time I made sure of you."

She didn't understand that last statement, but there was no time to argue. Gray lowered his head to cover her mouth with his own. There was a new element in this kiss, Amber vaguely realized. It was a deeply sensual demand that she had never before encountered. It fascinated her, drew her deeper into the seductive web of excitement building between them. Their lips clung as they learned the taste of each other.

Amber trembled in anticipation as Gray's big hands slid slowly down her back. He molded her to him, making her intoxicatingly aware of every hard line of his body. Luxuriating in the feel of him, she tangled her fingers in the thickness of his hair and then she traced the line of his neck down to the smooth, muscled contours of his shoulders. It felt so good to be held by him, she thought dazedly. Her nails sank briefly into the fabric of his shirt, and she sighed against his mouth.

Gray released her lips at last to nuzzle the scented area behind her ear. He twisted one hand in her hair and gently pulled her head back so that he had access to the sweetly vulnerable hollow of her throat.

"You're so soft and warm and exciting." His voice was dark with the coiling tendrils of masculine desire. "I don't know how I waited this long."

"Gray." She said his name with a thrill of possessive need that would have startled her under ordinary circumstances. As it was, she was only distantly aware of whispering the single, aching word. Gray was sliding his palms up under the hem of the peasant blouse, lifting the fabric away from her breasts.

"Raise your arms, my love."

Obediently she did so, and he removed the blouse entirely. Underneath she had worn no bra or camisole. For a moment Amber experienced a shaft of uncertainty. Gray had never seen her like this, never touched her as he would in the next few minutes. But the look in his eyes was infinitely reassuring. She knew with a woman's sure instinct that he was very satisfied with the sight of her small, firm breasts. He groaned softly and lightly ran his fingers across one nipple. Instantly the rosy peak hardened beneath his touch.

"What's the matter, sweetheart?" he asked gently as she buried her head against his shoulder.

"Nothing. I was just thinking that by the time most people get married they know each other much more intimately than we do."

"You mean that they've either gone to bed together or come very close to it. Worried about rude surprises? Are you afraid you won't like what you see when you take off my shirt?"

"Don't laugh at me, Gray. You know very well that's not what I meant." She lifted her head and smiled sheepishly. "But maybe I was a little scared you'd be disappointed in me. After all, you haven't... I mean you didn't get a chance to, uh, really see me before tonight."

"I've seen you a hundred times in my dreams," he told her deliberately. "But the reality is turning out to be far better than the dream. You're very, very lovely."

Amber murmured an odd sounding, very polite little thank-you into his shirt, and he laughed tenderly as he pulled her close. Feeling far more sure of herself now, Amber began unbuttoning the embroidered Acapulco-style shirt he wore. When his broad chest was exposed to her touch, she found herself thoroughly entranced by the crisp, curling dark hair that formed a wide vee, which tapered down to the waistband of his slacks.

"Will I do?" Gray asked thickly.

"You're perfect," she whispered dreamily. Her fingertips laced through his chest hair until she found the small, flat nipples. There she paused to explore and was rewarded by Gray's heavily sucked-in breath.

He quickly found the fastening of her flounced skirt and undid it. The turquoise garment fell to the floor in a frothy heap, leaving Amber in her cream satin panties. Gray wrapped his palms around the soft curves of her buttocks and squeezed gently. She was urged into the heat of his own thighs, and Amber trembled again in reaction. Then Gray slid his fingers under the panties and pushed them slowly down over her hips. When they fell to her ankles, Amber stepped out of them and out of her sandals.

The heated gold in Gray's gaze was all she needed to overcome the last, brief moment of uncertainty Amber felt as she stood completely nude before him. Then he was scooping her up in his arms and carrying her to the wide bed.

He stood her on her feet for a moment while he reached down to yank back the bedclothes. Then Gray set her carefully down on the snowy sheets. There was a deep intensity in him as he looked down at her. Amber could feel invisible bonds reaching out to ensnare her and ignite tiny flames along her nerve endings. Under that green-gold gaze she felt very beautiful, very sensual, truly desired and wonderfully cherished. She'd never experienced such a combination of emotions.

Gray sat down on a chair near the bed and pulled off his shoes with careless impatience. Then he rose, his fingers going to the buckle of his belt. His eyes never left Amber's flushed face as he stepped out of the remainder of his clothing.

Fascinated by the sheer male power in him, Amber's eyes moved down the length of his solid, smoothly muscled frame. The broad angles of his chest tapered into a lean, taut waist. Below that the lines of his hips and thighs were as solid and hard as the rest of him. The evidence of his arousal was boldly visible. Amber felt a primitive thrill run through her as she came to terms with the fact that this man was hers and that he wanted her every bit as much as she wanted him. She raised her eyes to his and held out her hand in a gesture of ancient, feminine welcome.

"*Amber*. My sweet, hot, beautiful Amber." Gray came down beside her on the bed, stilling her shifting legs with one of his own heavy thighs. He caught her wrists and laced his fingers through hers. Pinning her hands gently to the pillow on either side of her head, he leaned over and kissed her with an achingly deep demand.

Amber responded without hesitation, her mouth opening for his in silent acknowledgment of her own desire. She was lost in the wonder of the moment. No thoughts of the past or the future intruded to distract or dismay. She and this man belonged together tonight. The energy and excitement and throbbing need

that was driving both of them did not allow for any ex-
traneous memories or concerns.

Amber moaned softly as Gray's tongue found hers
and began a primitive duel that sent hot flames of desire through her. She gasped when she felt the slight,
teasing touch of his teeth on her lower lip. Then he was
withdrawing from her mouth to seek the curves of
throat, shoulder and breast with hungry kisses.

Gray freed her hands as he worked his way slowly,
lingeringly down her body. He covered one breast with
his palm as he tenderly took the opposite nipple between his teeth.

Amber whispered his name aloud far back in her
throat, and her fingertips dug into the skin of his
shoulders. She loved the feel of him, gloried in his
strength. The weight of him along the length of her
body was a heady, arousing caress in itself. It made her
twist and shiver beneath him.

"You're so exciting," Gray muttered fiercely as his
hand slid down to curve around her hip. "Just the feel
of you is enough to drive me over the edge. You're so
responsive. It's like holding hot silver in my hands. No,
I take that back." His smile was sensual. "Liquid Amber."

"Oh, Gray, I can't believe this. I've never felt anything like it." She lifted herself against his hand as he
delicately stroked the inside of her thigh. The intimate
touch made her moan softly again, and Gray was
pleased by her reaction.

"This is new for me, too," he rasped against the silky
skin of her hip. "I'm not sure I believe it, either. I've
waited so long." He used his teeth again, this time in a
fragile, teasing little nip that sent another burst of excitement through Amber. She reacted at once, trying

to curl into him. She got one leg free and curved it enticingly around his thigh.

"Please, Gray," she pleaded in a gentle, seductive voice that carried all her aching need. "Please come to me now. I want you so."

He raised his head to look up at her as if he was seeking confirmation of her words in her expression. Whatever he saw must have satisfied him, Amber thought. He touched the dampening warmth between her legs until she was crying out and clinging to him and then Gray came to her.

He settled himself along the length of her eager body, parting her legs with his own. She inhaled deeply when she felt the waiting hardness of him probing gently at the damp, heated place between her legs. Her fingers clenched in his hair as she realized just how massive and solid he really was. Gray paused, aware of the slight hesitation in her.

"Amber?" His voice was raw with the effort it took to control his passion.

"It's all right," she said, urging him closer. "I just hadn't realized. I mean, you're quite large all over, aren't you?"

"Sweetheart." He groaned, burying his face in her hair. "Honey, I don't want to hurt you. I'll be very careful with you." His body was tight with the need he was holding so severely in check.

Amber smiled the secret smile that only another woman could ever understand and let her nails sink deeper into his strong shoulders. "Not too careful, I hope."

"*Amber.*" He reacted at once to the teasing bite of her nails and the feminine urging in her voice. With a heavy, powerful thrust, Gray sank himself into Amber's softness. He held her in bonds of steel and velvet, waiting for her body to adjust to his.

"Yes," she gasped into his ear. "Oh, yes, Gray."

"So good," he muttered, the words dark and husky and laden with thick desire. "You feel so damn good."

Slowly then, he began to move within her. She lifted herself into each of his thrusts, drawing him deeper, clinging to him with her legs and arms and the small muscles inside her body. Instinctively she held him as tightly as possible. Gray wrapped her securely in his arms, his heavy frame covered hers completely as she sought to give herself up to the leaping excitement.

Together they pursued the driving rhythm. Amber's head twisted on the pillow, her eyes closed, her lips slightly parted as she strove for the satisfaction that tantalized and beckoned.

"That's it, my love," Gray said. "Take it. It's all yours. Come and take it, Amber." He lifted himself slightly away from her, just far enough so that he could slip one hand between their bodies.

Amber's breath caught in her throat as she felt him stroke the most sensitive part of her and then she cried out as he surged into her one more time. The splintering climax swirled outward, taking her completely. She surrendered to it with a sense of wonder and awe, holding tightly to the man who had made it possible.

Even as the tiny, exquisite ripples of sensation began to fade, Amber heard Gray say her name between clenched teeth. His hands clutched heavily on her shoulders, and his body went tense. Then he, too, was giving himself up to the spinning moment of release. Together they rode it until the storm subsided and then they collapsed in each other's arms.

Slowly Gray returned to the present, aware of Amber's satiny, damp warmth. Her eyes were still closed with a lazy contentment, and there was a fine sheen of perspiration between her breasts. She lay entwined in his arms as if she had no wish to be anywhere else in the world at that moment.

He lifted himself carefully, reluctantly away from her and smiled when she murmured a small protest without opening her eyes. "Come here," he invited indulgently as he gathered her against him. "Curl up and go to sleep."

She obeyed him with a small sigh of trust and pleasure. Gray stroked the curve of her hip with a sense of deep satisfaction as he watched her drift off to sleep in his arms.

It was almost amusing to know that she had thought herself incapable of reacting so passionately to him. The only thing that kept it from being genuinely humorous was that her careful, polite conviction had deprived him of her presence in his bed for nearly three months.

He'd told himself he wanted to wait until she acknowledged her own desires and he'd been right. Tomorrow morning she would wake with the knowledge that she was not only capable of a passionate response to her new husband but that she had actively precipitated the lovemaking.

It would be good for her to come to terms with that, Gray decided. He would be careful not to force her to admit it aloud just yet, however. He sensed she would still need time. For too long she had convinced herself she would never be able to fall deeply, passionately in love. Whatever that man in California had done to her, he had managed to lock her in ice for over six months.

He had made her afraid of her own strong passions and that was a crime for which Gray would have very much liked to exact punishment.

On the other hand, Gray told himself as he yawned widely, if it hadn't been for the jerk in California, he would never have met Amber. Now that Amber had set herself free at last, it was hard to maintain a grudge against the unknown male who had traumatized her.

Gray fell asleep wondering how long it would take Amber to admit to herself and to him the full significance of what had happened between them.

AMBER AWOKE THE NEXT MORNING with a languid sense of contentment. She stirred and stretched out her foot, seeking Gray's leg. When she didn't find it, she opened her eyes and peered inquiringly around the hotel room. She didn't see her husband, but she could hear the sound of water running in the shower. A glance at the clock on the bedside table showed that it was nearly eight. Patting back a small yawn, she kicked off the covers and got to her feet.

Her first reaction to the small, interesting aches in her body was one of surprise. Then she grinned ruefully and stretched. Gray was definitely not a lightweight. Any woman who shared his bed was going to remember the occasion. Amber reminded herself cheerfully that she was the woman who had the right to share Gray's bed and then she strolled toward the bathroom.

The steam rolled out in great clouds as she opened the door and called Gray's name. "Good morning," she said into the mist. "What's going on in here? Are you taking a steam bath?"

"Come in and find out," he invited. His big hand grasped the shower curtain and pulled it aside. Through the heavy atmosphere, he appraised the naked length of her body and grinned. "I was wondering when you'd wake up. It's getting late, and we've still got to make our way back to Washington today. Quit stalling, woman, and get into the shower."

She felt the pink rise into her cheeks as she submitted to his devastatingly frank examination. Amber hoped he would assume the color in her face was caused by the steam from the shower. She raised one brow at the sardonic, very male expression on his face and stepped forward with a saucy boldness. It was a new sensation. She'd never felt this distinctly feminine sort of smugness before in her life.

When she was within reaching distance, she treated Gray to the same deliberate appraisal he had given her. "Not bad," she said with mocking thoughtfulness. "I'll admit I expected a little something more this morning given the fact that you've had the whole night to recover. But don't worry about it. I'm perfectly content to take quality over quantity. And I certainly understand that as men grow older they tend to go for quality rather than quantity in certain areas."

"Why, you insatiable little hussy," he growled. "Come here and say that again." He wrapped one large hand around the nape of her neck and hauled her easily into the shower. Amber screeched as she was instantly drenched and then she was laughing up at him as he steadied her against his wet, slippery frame. Gray assumed a stern expression. "I decided to play the gentleman this morning and let you sleep since you were obviously so thoroughly exhausted from last night. Perfectly understandable, your being a member of the weaker sex and all. But if a lot of sass is all my fine behavior is going to earn me, I might as well forget the good manners and enjoy myself."

"Please do," she said, her eyes brimming with anticipation. She wound her arms around his neck as he lifted her against the hardening outline of his hips. The sassy teasing went out of her as Gray joined their bodies with a strong movement that left Amber gasping in his firm hold. He held her high against him. She circled his waist with her legs and clung to him as the water cascaded over both of them.

This time the passion was very quick, swamping them almost immediately and leaving them breathless in its wake. When it was over, Gray lowered Amber carefully to her feet and steadied her as she found her balance.

"Good grief," she complained with exaggerated surprise as she leaned against him. "No more cracks about quantity versus quality, I promise. I'm not sure I'd survive too many demonstrations like the last one."

He nuzzled her neck, his laughter silent and deep. "Don't underestimate yourself. I'm sure that with proper coaching and practice you'll soon be able to keep up with me."

"I think I hear a touch of masculine ego talking here."

"Of course you do. After all, I'm a male and I've got an ego. You're bound to find yourself dealing with it on occasion," Gray informed her blandly as he picked up the soap and began lathering her body.

"I'll remember that," she vowed, and gave herself up to the intimate luxury of being bathed by her husband.

It wasn't until they were on the jet bound for the Seattle area airport that Gray casually mentioned the party.

"What party?" Amber put down the magazine she had been reading and gave him a questioning glance.

"I think we should have one, don't you? I'm not big on large social events, but in this case I can see a purpose. I want to introduce you to my friends and clients as my wife. Some of them have already met you, of course, but I want to make everything official. Surely you have a few friends you'd like to invite?"

Amber thought of her sister and brother-in-law as well as a few of the people she had met since she had moved to Washington. "Well, yes, I imagine I could find a couple of people to invite. Are you sure you want to go to all this bother, Gray?"

He gave her an odd look. "As I said, it has a purpose."

"Introducing me as your wife?" She shrugged. "All right. I don't mind giving a party. Might be fun."

"I have a particularly good friend living in Vancouver," Gray went on thoughtfully, "but I don't think I'll ask him and his wife to come down to Bellevue for the party. This event will be largely business oriented, and I'd rather see Mitch and Lacey on a more casual basis."

"Mitch and Lacey?"

He nodded. "Their last name is Evans. One of these days we'll drive up to Vancouver and spend a weekend with them. You'll like them. I know they're going to be curious about you."

Amber picked up her magazine again, but she didn't see the words on the page. Instead, she started thinking ahead to the party she and Gray would be giving. It was a very *married* thing to do, she realized. When a husband and wife gave a party together, the act had a way of emphasizing the relationship between the host and hostess. In the eyes of the friends and business associates who would be gathered in Gray's home, it would serve to set a seal on the marriage. She and Gray would definitely be viewed as a couple—a married couple.

Amber put the magazine down once more and gazed out the window. She and Gray were truly married now. Their relationship was no longer in limbo. There were lovers as well as friends.

*Lovers.* The word came into her mind, haunted her for a short time and then retreated to the edges of her thoughts. She tried to keep it out of sight while she attempted once more to read, but a few minutes later it wove its way back into her consciousness.

She hoped she had made Gray happy last night. She was certain he had been fully satisfied. That was only right and proper, Amber told herself firmly. He was a good man and a good husband. He deserved whatever physical satisfaction she could give him.

The truth was, she admitted silently, she had enjoyed pleasing him. No, there was more to it than that. She had found her own pleasure in his arms, too. He had given himself as freely and completely as she had given herself to him. There was no reason to deny the reaction they'd had to each other. After all, she was committed to the marriage. If they couldn't take satisfaction in each other's arms, they would be contemplating a pretty dismal future this morning. A husband and a wife had a right to find contentment in bed with each other.

Amber decided to let it go at that. She didn't want to pursue the logic of her thoughts any farther. She and Gray would be content with each other, and that was enough. It was a good deal more than most couples had. Gray seemed satisfied with the relationship, and there was no reason Amber shouldn't be equally satisfied.

Determinedly she picked up the magazine yet again, unaware of the speculative gleam in Gray's sidelong glance.

When he saw her return to her reading at last, Gray went back to the article he had been perusing. He couldn't read her mind, but he could make a damn good guess about what she was thinking. He also knew from the slight frown between her brows that she wasn't altogether sure of her conclusions.

She wasn't regretting last night, he decided. But perhaps she was beginning to wonder just why she had found it so easy to surrender to her new husband. Perhaps she was telling herself that a certain degree of physical pleasure was only to be expected under the circumstances. After all, she and Gray were friends. They liked each other, shared a similar sense of humor and were physically compatible. There was no reason to be terribly surprised to discover they dealt well together in bed.

But there had been a great deal more than pleasant physical gratification between them last night, Gray thought. He wondered how long it would take Amber to realize it. He wondered how long it would take Amber to realize that she was truly his wife and that she was bound to him by a great deal more than just a legal document and a pleasant working relationship that extended into bed.

TEN DAYS LATER Amber stood in front of the wide expanse of windows that framed the living room of Gray's house and wondered if she'd overlooked any last-minute details. The guests were due to start arriving at any moment.

The buffet tables had been set with great care. They bore an elaborate and interesting assortment of pâtés, hors d'oeuvres, crackers, cheeses, fresh fruits and spreads. Extra dishes of nearly everything waited in the kitchen to be brought out as needed. A fully stocked bar had been set up at the far end of the room where Gray would play the generous host. The view from the windows would provide a spectacular backdrop to the gathering. It all looked quite graciously inviting.

Amber frowned at her own image in the mirrors that reflected the view of the lake. Her hair was caught up in an artful twist that gave her a more sophisticated look than she normally favored. She was wearing a new dress tonight, one Gray had helped her select. It was fashioned of heavy flame-red silk and was cinched at the waist with a wide belt. There was a dazzling yellow border print around the hem and a rakish collar that framed her throat. The dress did not show a lot of surplus skin for all its dash and charm. Gray had rejected all the offerings that featured off-the-shoulder or deepneckline styling. Amber was beginning to realize that he'd meant what he'd said about being possessive. She grimaced wryly in the mirror at the thought.

"Everything okay?"

She swung around, the red silk whipping gracefully about her calves. Gray stood in the doorway surveying the room and her. He was wearing an expensive but conservatively cut white shirt and a pair of dark slacks. His jacket was light in color, emphasizing his strong build. Amber smiled and walked across the floor to fiddle with his dark tie.

"Everything appears to be in perfect order," she assured him. "I just hope someone shows up. We'd have a hard time eating all this food by ourselves."

"Don't worry." He laughed, tipping her face up for a brief kiss. "Someone will show. I think we can count on your sister for certain."

"Ummm. You're right. She knows I'd strangle her if she didn't appear. Finish the final report for Symington?"

Gary nodded. "Almost. I learned long ago not to hurry these things. Clients are afraid they didn't get their money's worth if I don't spend a sufficient amount of time on the project. I should wait at least another week before I mail the final report."

"Even though you're going to recommend against the purchase?"

"Especially since I'm going to recommend against the purchase. When you're advising someone to turn down a big deal like this, you want to make them think you really gave it grave consideration."

Amber grinned. "You don't want Symington to know you took one good look at the books, examined the golf course and the wine cellar and said to hell with the whole thing?"

"Psychology, my dear," he reminded her blandly. "We must never forget the psychological element in business."

She batted her eyes in mock admiration. "I can't believe how much I'm learning from you these days."

"Pay attention. It gets more interesting." He gave her a knowing look that brought a vivid flush to her cheeks.

"I'm not sure I can stand too much education," she managed to retort, remembering last night's sensual lesson. Gray had been feeling quite adventurous, she recalled with amusement. She had found herself on the carpet in front of the floor-to-ceiling mirrors that lined one bedroom wall. It had been more than interesting. It had been wildly exhilarating.

"Who was educating whom last night?" he asked wryly. "It wasn't me who started quoting Sherborne Ulysses Twitchell in the middle of things."

"Somehow it just seemed appropriate," Amber murmured, her eyes sparkling with wicked amusement. Even now she didn't want to examine too closely just why she had sought refuge in sexy humor last night. She had been shatteringly aware of standing on the edge of an emotional cliff in Gray's arms. It was as if she had looked down from the mountaintop and seen the mists that shielded the valley floor parting for the first time. She had been afraid to look over the edge any longer, afraid to see the truth that awaited her. It had been much easier to step back and find another outlet for her heady emotions. She had summoned up a line from Twitchell, and both she and Gray had collapsed into laughter.

"Twitchell is always appropriate of course," Gray assured her. "But I swear if you bring up one more reference to heavy, smoking iron when I have you in the position I had you in last night, I'm going to take drastic action."

"You did take drastic action," she answered, unperturbed. "Speaking of hot iron, that reminds me. You should be receiving your next copy of *Radiant Sunsets* any day now. I can't wait to read Honoria Tyler Abercrombie's article on phallic symbols."

The light of battle came to life in Gray's eyes. "Ms Abercrombie is going to rue the day she challenged me in print."

"We'll see." Amber turned away with a last teasing smile as the doorbell chimed. "Ah, our first guests. We're not going to have to eat all this food alone after all." She walked toward the door with Gray at her side.

Fifteen minutes after the first guests had arrived, Cynthia and Sam Paxton parked their BMW in the driveway and came toward the steps. Amber had just been about to close the door after the guests who had preceded her sister. When she glanced out and saw who was arriving, she left the Wilsons to Gray's care and went to meet Cynthia and Sam.

"Cynthia, you look great." She hugged her sister affectionately, startled by the tension in the other woman's body. "Hi, Sam," she added quickly to the good-looking, rusty-haired man standing beside Cynthia. "It's good to see you again. Come on inside."

"Go on, Sam, I'll be along in a minute. I want to have a quick word with Amber," Cynthia announced.

"Sure. See you in a minute, Amber." He sauntered off to say hello to Gray, who was back at the door.

When they were alone, Amber turned to her sister with concern. "What's wrong, Cyn?"

"Everything," Cynthia declared in grim tones. She searched her sister's face anxiously. "He's here, Amber. Right here in Bellevue. He came to see me yesterday trying to find you."

A cold premonition crystallized deep in Amber's stomach. "Who are you talking about, Cynthia?"

"Roarke Kelley," Cynthia exclaimed impatiently. "He's been hurt in a race accident, and he's come looking for you to soothe his fevered brow."

"Oh, my God."

Cynthia sighed. "I had a hunch you'd say something like that."

## 7

AMBER ASKED THE FIRST QUESTION that came into her head. "Did you tell him where I live now?"

"No," Cynthia assured her quickly. "But it's not going to take him long to find you. You know that. He'll go to your old apartment and ask a few questions. That's all it's going to require for him to locate you."

Amber shook her head, feeling dazed. "But why should he want to find me, Cyn? He was the one who broke things off between us."

"Not exactly," Cynthia retorted. "As I recall the story, you finally informed him you'd had enough and that you didn't want to see him again."

"Well, he certainly didn't give me any argument on the subject," Amber said feelingly. "He was involved with a blonde at the time. I got the impression he wasn't even aware I'd made our breakup official."

"He's very good-looking, isn't he?" Cynthia said musingly as she and Amber turned to walk slowly toward the house. "I hadn't realized. I mean, I hadn't met him while you were dating him, and I just had no idea he was quite so attractive. Lots of dark, brooding, wicked good looks. And then there's that dashing touch of danger racing lends him. No wonder you were swept off your feet."

"What an intolerable situation." Amber ignored what her sister was saying as she tried to think of how to handle the problem that confronted her. "Why the hell did he have to show up?" She pictured Roarke Kelley in her mind and groaned. "Was he badly hurt, Cyn?"

"He's got an interesting scar or two, but that's about all I could see. They just add to his attraction. Rather like old-fashioned dueling scars, if you know what I mean. He didn't say much about the accident, just enough to imply he had suffered bravely. I only talked to him for a few minutes. I got rid of him as quickly as I could."

"Did you tell him I was married?"

"Those were practically the first words out of my mouth," Cynthia assured her.

"Did the news put him off, do you think?" Amber realized she felt numb. She couldn't seem to think straight. The thought of facing a room full of Gray's business friends was suddenly overwhelming.

Cynthia shook her head. "I don't think your marriage fazed him in the least. If so, he didn't show it."

"He wouldn't," Amber said miserably. "He'll probably see it as a challenge. Oh, Lord, Cynthia, what am I going to do?"

"Tell Gray?" Cynthia suggested quietly.

"No! Absolutely not!" Amber was shocked at the suggestion. "I don't want Gray involved in this. It's my problem. I'll have to take care of Roarke on my own."

"Why? You've got a husband now. Let him help you."

"Cynthia, I have no idea how Gray would react to this. We've only been married two weeks. He might be very upset. He might be hurt. He would most definitely be shocked. What husband wouldn't be? I've never told him about Roarke. He knows I was involved with someone in California and that the experience left a bad taste in my mouth, but that's all he knows. Regardless of how he might feel about the situation, I'm an adult woman. I have to handle my own past."

Cynthia looked unconvinced. "I'm not so sure, Amber. I like Gray."

"So do I. That's one of the reasons I don't want him to have to confront Roarke for me," Amber said swiftly.

Cynthia eyed her sister curiously. "You *like* Gray?"

"Well, of course I do, idiot. I wouldn't have married him otherwise. I am very content with Gray."

"Content? I was hoping that after two weeks of marriage you might have decided that what you felt for Gray involved more than just a sense of contentment."

Amber was startled. "I happen to appreciate the state of being content," she said bluntly. "I assure you, I'm totally committed to this marriage, Cynthia. But we've only been married two weeks. I'm not about to risk everything I've begun to build with Gray by throwing Roarke Kelley at him and telling him to do something about the man. I'm going to have to deal with this myself." Amber broke off for a moment as they reached the front door. "Maybe Roarke will just give up and go away," she said hopefully.

"I wouldn't count on it," Cynthia said frankly. "He came a long way looking for you. He's not likely to just disappear without trying his hand at seducing you. You said yourself you're probably a challenge to him now."

Amber paled. "Seducing me?" She repeated the words with a kind of stunned horror.

"You don't think he's come all this way just to wish you good luck in your marriage, do you?" Cynthia asked pointedly.

Amber couldn't think of anything to say to that. She opened the door with a sense of impending doom and found Gray standing on the other side. Frantically she summoned up her best reassure-the-client smile.

"I was just about to go outside and see what was keeping you," he said quietly. His green-and-gold eyes moved over her too-bright expression with lazy appraisal.

"Amber and I were just having a quick sisterly chat," Cynthia told him smoothly. "I haven't had much chance to talk to her since she got back from her honeymoon, and I knew we wouldn't get much of an opportunity tonight. What a crowd! Did the two of you prepare all this food?"

"Amber supervised. I just followed orders. Turns out she cooks better than she types." Gray held out his hand to his wife. "Come with me, honey. I want to introduce you to some friends of mine."

Amber obediently gave him her hand, and he folded it inside his large, competent palm. She wondered if he was aware of how cold her fingers were. Hastily she regrouped her forces and plunged into her hostessing chores. "Have fun, Cynthia. Elizabeth Bead arrived a few minutes ago. She said she wanted to talk to you about your trip to Hawaii."

Cynthia smiled agreeably, darting a quick glance at Gray's impassively polite face. "I'll go find her. Nice to see you again, Gray."

He nodded and with a firm grip led Amber toward a small knot of people standing by the window. "Did your sister say something to upset you?"

Amber caught her breath and then smiled even more brilliantly. "Oh, no. She just wanted to tell me about something that happened to her yesterday. I gather she had an unexpected guest."

"Is everything all right?"

"Just fine. I didn't get all the details." *Good heavens*, Amber thought in mounting horror. *I've got to shut up. I'm actually on the verge of lying to him. I can't lie to Gray.* Frantically she changed the subject. "Who are these people I'm about to meet? Anyone I should pretend to know by reputation?"

"MacKenzie would be thrilled if you told him you'd heard of his restaurant chain plans," Gray said, sounding amused.

"Well, I can say that, can't I? I just heard about them from you."

"Do you always tell the truth, Amber?" Gray asked as if academically interested in the question.

"Certainly." She paused. "If I can." He knew something was wrong. She was going to have to be very careful tonight.

"Have you always told me the truth?"

Her eyes flew to his. "Always," she vowed.

"But sometimes you choose not to answer questions."

"Everyone has the right not to answer certain questions," she declared staunchly. She knew he was thinking about that afternoon when they'd had lunch in the canyon and he'd asked her about her past. "That's not the same thing as lying."

"No," he agreed gently, "it's not."

There was no time for him to say anything else. They had reached the convivial group by the window, and Gray introduced his wife with a quiet male pride that made Amber more determined than ever not to involve him in the situation she faced with Roarke Kelley. She would not allow Roarke to jeopardize her marriage, and she knew him well enough to know that he was not above trying to do exactly that; not because he was passionately in love with her, but simply to repay her for bruising his ego six months ago. Roarke was generally the one who ended relationships. He wasn't accustomed to having a woman return the favor as Amber had done.

She had to get rid of Kelley, she told herself a hundred times that evening as she played the role of wife and hostess and business partner. She didn't want to see him, but there would probably be no way to avoid it. She couldn't let him track her down and just show up on her doorstep.

The nervous tension built steadily within her all evening. Amber thought she covered it reasonably well and hoped that if anyone noticed her edginess he or she would chalk it up to the excitement and the pressure of giving her first major party with Gray. She knew Cynthia was concerned about her, but apparently Sam knew nothing of the day's events. He was as blithely friendly and genial as ever. Gray seemed to like him, which was nice, Amber told herself.

By eleven o'clock Amber was beginning to wonder if the party would ever end. She knew she was never going to remember all the names of Gray's business associates. Even if her full attention had been concentrated on the task, she probably couldn't have managed that trick. As it was, she would be lucky to remember a fraction of them. All evening long her mind kept darting back and forth between the looming problem of Roarke Kelley and the pressure of trying to maintain a charming facade for Gray's friends and associates. It took all her stamina to survive with a smile on her face until the door finally closed behind the last guest.

"Well, that's over," Gray said in relieved satisfaction as he locked the door. He absently began loosening the knot of his tie as he strolled toward Amber. "You looked a little harried there at times. How are you feeling?"

"Exhausted." It was nothing less than the truth. Anxiously she met his eyes. "Did I really look harried? Do you think any of your guests noticed?"

He shook his head slowly, smiling at her. But his eyes were watchful, and Amber's nerves tightened another notch. "Relax. You did a beautiful job. I was very proud of you. I imagine it showed."

She returned his smile, relaxing for an instant in the knowledge that he was pleased with her. "Yes, it showed. But it works both ways, you know. I'm sure everyone here tonight was well aware of how proud I am of you."

He slipped the tie from around his neck and slung it over his shoulder as he walked toward her. Amber wished desperately she could tell what he was thinking. There was a slight smile edging his mouth, but it didn't quite compensate for the almost analytical look in his eyes. "Are you proud of me, Amber?" Gray asked curiously.

Her eyes widened in surprise at the question. Impulsively she went into his arms. "Definitely. I feel very fortunate to be married to you. I wasn't sure at first that we were doing the right thing by getting married, but now I'm very glad I let you talk me into it."

He framed her face between his wide palms. His thumbs traced the line of her jaw with subdued sensuality as Gray gazed thoughtfully down into her upturned face. "You're happy with me?"

"Oh, yes, Gray. Very happy." *And I'll do whatever I have to do to protect that happiness,* Amber added with silent conviction. She searched his gaze, wondering what had prompted him to start asking such questions tonight of all times. "What about you? Are you happy?"

He nodded seriously. "Yes," he said simply. "I think things are working out all right."

Amber's laugh was a little shaky. "What's that supposed to mean?"

His eyes grew more intent as he lowered his head to kiss her. "I'll tell you one of these days."

She wanted to ask him to explain, but his mouth was claiming hers, and right at that moment Amber was overcome by a fierce need to be held as only Gray could hold her. Throwing her arms around his neck, she pressed herself passionately against him, deepening the kiss with a kind of wild abandon that seemed to take Gray by surprise for an instant.

But he wasn't about to interrupt the new mood by asking any more questions. In a gesture of easy strength, he cradled Amber in his arms and carried her down the hall and into the bedroom. There in the shadows Amber drew him down into an embrace that left them both trembling and deliciously exhausted. Held tenderly in his arms, Amber found the reassurance and sense of safety she needed so desperately that night.

SEATED AT HIS DESK across the room from Amber the next morning, Gray covertly eyed his wife. Something was wrong, and it was clear she wasn't ready yet to tell him about it. Logic told him it had something to do with whatever she and her sister had been discussing last night. Short of pinning Amber down and demanding an explanation, Gray didn't see how he was going to find out what was going on. Whatever it was, Amber had apparently decided to handle it herself.

That alarmed him.

In the first place, he told himself, she should be coming to him for help if she was in any kind of trouble. In the second place, he worried that, whatever the problem was, Amber might worsen it or complicate things by trying to deal with it on her own.

He'd already had a taste of her bravery. He would never forget that night she had boldly come to his rescue by pretending to be his bodyguard. She still didn't know just how much danger she had been in that night. The lady had guts, but he wasn't sure just how much common sense she had to go along with them. There was more passion and impulsiveness in her than she herself realized.

Gray watched her sip her third cup of tea. That action alone was cause for concern. Amber normally only had one cup in the morning and one in the afternoon. It wasn't yet eleven o'clock, and here she was on her third. He thought about telling her that whatever had put her nerves on edge, caffeine wasn't going to help. Then he decided against it. She didn't look as though she was in the mood for advice.

"I'll have to leave for that luncheon meeting with Harrison soon," Gray said quietly into the stillness.

Amber's head came up with a jerk as if he'd just shouted at her. Belatedly she smiled. "Yes, that's right. I'd almost forgotten. Still expect to be gone for most of the afternoon?"

Gray nodded. Such meetings weren't unusual. Amber was accustomed to having the house and the office to herself when he was meeting clients. "Had any more thoughts about Harrison's project?"

She blinked as if the Harrison job had been the farthest thing from her mind that morning. Gray could almost see her struggling to pull her scattered thoughts together.

"No, not really. I agree with you that if he insists on buying that software firm he'll be taking too big a risk. It's a real gamble, given the status of the software market at the moment, but I know Harrison has dreams of making his fortune in a hurry. You probably won't be able to talk him out of the deal. Therefore you might as well take him on as a client. You might be able to help him avoid some of the larger pitfalls he's bound to encounter."

"That's what I like about you, Amber. You have a nice, practical approach to this business." He smiled at her.

"Well, I knew you didn't keep me around for three months because of my phenomenal skill at the typewriter," she managed to retort with a trace of her usual flippant humor.

Gray got to his feet and walked over to kiss her lightly on the nose. "You're absolutely right. I didn't keep you on as my assistant because of your typing skill. There were a whole lot of other reasons. One of these days I'll tell you about them. Right now, I'd better dig out a tie and jacket for lunch. Sure you don't want to come along?"

Amber shook her head quickly. "You don't need me, and I have a lot of things to do today."

"All right. I'll see you late this afternoon. Goodbye, honey."

Amber sighed with relief a few minutes later as she watched Gray walk out the door and climb into his slightly staid Mercedes. She had been sitting on pins and needles all morning long wondering when the phone would ring. She was a nervous wreck anticipating having to deal with Roarke Kelley. The thought of having to handle him while Gray listened in on the conversation had been enough to induce an anxiety attack.

She closed the front door after seeing Gray off and traipsed back to the office. There she flung herself into her chair and gazed moodily out the window.

Perhaps Roarke wouldn't call. Perhaps he wouldn't be able to find her as easily as Cynthia seemed to think. Perhaps he would leave town without contacting her now that he knew Amber was married.

All three possibilities were false hopes, and deep in the pit of her stomach Amber's nerves told her not to believe in any of them. If Roarke had come this far to see her, he wasn't likely to simply give up and go away without making contact.

Twenty minutes later the phone rang. Amber jumped, her attention wrenched from the financial report she had been attempting to study. With a sense of doom she picked up the receiver. Her instincts told her who it would be before she even said hello.

"Amber?" Roarke's voice was low and sexy and intimate. It had always been that way. He'd probably been born with the kind of vocal cords that automatically produced low, sexy, intimate sounds. "It's been a long time, honey. Too long."

"Not long enough, Roarke." For some reason now that the anticipated moment was finally upon her, Amber felt suddenly more in control. Worrying about a problem was always worse than actually dealing with it. Her fingers tightened around the receiver. She could handle Roarke Kelley. Damn it, she *would* handle him.

"You don't sound surprised to hear from me. Did your sister tell you I was looking for you?"

"She told me. But I'm not interested in seeing you, Roarke." Amber hesitated and then stated baldly, "I'm married."

"On the rebound, Amber?" he asked softly.

Amber shut her eyes in silent dismay. Secretly she had been hoping that the word *married* would act as some sort of talisman to ward off Roarke. She should have known it wouldn't even slow him down. He'd had more than one affair with a married woman according to the bits and pieces of racetrack gossip she'd garnered during the time she had been involved with him. "No, not on the rebound. What do you want, Roarke?"

"To see you."

"I don't see any point in that."

"I can come out to his house, if you like. I know where it is, Amber."

She caught her breath at the unsubtle threat, and for a moment she panicked. The thought of Gray opening the door to Roarke Kelley shook her. "For God's sake, Roarke, you can't come here!"

"Then meet me for lunch today," he returned calmly.

"Why?" she demanded.

"You want reasons?" he asked with sudden, harsh emotion. "Okay, I'll give you reasons. For the sake of what we once had. Because we never had a chance to say goodbye properly. Because I nearly bought the farm two months ago down in Florida, and I had a lot of time to think while waiting to see if I was ever going to drive again. I spent that time thinking about us, Amber. You, me and the future."

She was appalled. "Roarke, it's too late." She couldn't think of anything else to say. "Don't you understand? I'm married now. It's too late for you, me and the future. I think it was always too late for us."

"Is that why you jumped into marriage with the first man you found after me? Because you thought it was too late for us?"

"I didn't just jump into marriage, damn it. I've only been married a couple of weeks. Roarke, this conversation is pointless."

"I have to see you, honey. I've come too far and waited too long. I have to talk to you face-to-face one last time."

"No," she said with quiet firmness.

"Then I'll drive over to his house and see you there. I swear I will, Amber. I can't leave the state without talking to you. There are too many things I have to say. Things I should have said a long time ago."

Frantically Amber tried to think. "If I agree to see you one last time, will you give me your word you'll leave the area without making trouble, Roarke?"

"My word of honor."

What good had his word of honor ever been, Amber wondered in dismay. She didn't doubt he was honorable enough in his racing. He was practically a legend in those circles. But Roarke Kelley followed an entirely different code when it came to dealing with personal relationships. Still, perhaps if she saw him face-to-face she could convince him that she wasn't about to fall back into his palm like a ripe plum. "All right, Roarke. I'll meet you at noon under the clock in the shopping mall downtown."

"I don't want to meet you in some damn shopping mall."

"Why not? It's as good a meeting place as any other." She was not about to let him talk her into a rendezvous at some secluded restaurant or at his hotel. There was a certain degree of safety in a crowd. "There are a couple of good places to eat in the mall. I'll see you in half an hour. Goodbye, Roarke."

She hung up the phone before he could argue further. When she lifted her hand from the receiver, she realized her fingers were trembling. Still, she'd managed to fight the first round to a draw. She'd dictated the time and place of the meeting, even though she hadn't been able to avoid the confrontation itself. Resolutely Amber got to her feet. She could and would dictate the rest of what happened today between herself and Roarke.

Half an hour later she bravely walked into the crowded mall and headed for the agreed-upon meeting place. She saw Roarke almost at once. He was waiting for her, and he looked as devastatingly attractive as ever. The scar on his square jaw only added an element of dangerous intrigue to his already rakish persona. His black hair was in its usual endearing tousle. His vivid blue eyes were as riveting as ever. His lean body still moved with a languid, sensual grace. Roarke was dressed in a pair of light-colored pants, a wide leather belt, a T-shirt and a stylish, unconstructed jacket that fairly shouted Southern California machismo. Cynthia had been right. Roarke Kelley was wickedly good-looking. Even as she walked toward him, Amber was aware of other women turning their heads to take a second glance at Roarke. It had always been like that.

Amber took one look at him now and wondered what on earth she had ever seen in him. Frowning intently she went forward, aware that he was raking her snug, faded jeans and slouchy gold sweater with a deeply interested gaze. She hadn't bothered to dress for the event, and it showed. Her hair was in the same casual twist she'd had it in all morning. Amber hadn't even bothered to put on any lipstick. Roarke Kelley was accustomed to having his women look their best.

"Two weeks of marriage and already you look like Mrs. Average Housewife," he said bluntly as she came to a halt in front of him.

Amber took heart. "The operative part of that sentence is 'wife,'" she told him dryly. "Remember it."

"If you'd married me, you'd still be on your honeymoon," he said deliberately.

"Where? At a motel near some racetrack? Thanks, but no thanks. I don't know what you hoped to accomplish by insisting on this meeting, Roarke."

He stepped closer, his whole attention focused on her in that way he had that made a woman feel as though she were the only female in the universe. It was a special knack Roarke Kelley had. Women fell for it in droves, and Amber had been no exception at first. The lure of believing she was the one woman in the world who had the power to capture and reform the rake had trapped more than one intelligent woman. "Let's go someplace where we can have lunch."

"I'm not hungry."

"A cup of coffee then. Come on, Amber. I've come a long way to find you. I want to talk."

Amber groaned and swung around, heading for the nearest café. The place she chose featured buffet-style service. It was very busy and offered almost no intimacy. Roarke followed without a word, seating himself across from her with a cup of coffee. He was smiling knowingly as he looked into her eyes.

"You're afraid, aren't you?"

"Of what?"

"Of me. Of what will happen if you let yourself get too close to me again."

Amber didn't touch her coffee. She put both hands on the table and said in a low, cool tone, "Roarke, I want you to understand something. I'm going to spell this out as clearly as possible and when I'm finished I'm going to say goodbye. I'm married to a wonderful man, and I am totally committed to that marriage. Whatever you and I had between us is in the past and it's going to stay there. I don't know why you've come looking for me. You don't need or want me."

"That's not true, Amber. The accident made me realize that I do need and want you. It made me put my whole life into perspective. I was a fool to let you go six months ago. I want you back."

She shook her head slowly. "That's not possible, Roarke."

"Anything's possible."

She drew a deep breath. "You swore you would leave me alone if I agreed to see you today. I'm going to hold you to your word of honor, Roarke." Deliberately she emphasized *honor*.

He ignored it. "Are you happy, Amber?"

She flinched, remembering how Gray had asked her that very question just last night. "I don't see that it's any concern of yours, but yes, I'm happy. I'm quite content with my marriage, Roarke. You won't be able to lure me away from my husband."

"Content? That's not much of a word, is it?" he observed thoughtfully.

Quite suddenly Amber remembered how she'd felt playing bodyguard that night out on the desert. She'd known then that the only way to make the bluff work was to act very cool, very tough and very much in charge. Dealing with Roarke would require exactly the same facade. It was time to take the offensive.

"Do you want to hear just how content I am?" she asked with cold challenge. "I'll try to put this in words even you can understand. My husband is a strong man while you're weak in ways you don't even know about. You're bright and flashy, but my husband has a kind of emotional stamina and staying power you won't ever have. Your private, male code of honor is good on the racetrack, but you don't apply it anywhere else, therefore it's pretty useless. I have no respect for it. On the other hand, I could take my husband's sense of honor to the bank and use it for collateral on a loan. It's solid gold. You're physically attractive, but Gray is the kind of lover most women would kill for. Have I made myself clear? I am very, *very* content with my marriage. In fact, I will do whatever I have to do in order to protect it." Amber got to her feet. "Remember that, Roarke. Stay away from me."

She saw the dawning anger in his eyes, but she didn't wait for a response. Amber headed for the door without a backward glance. She'd used all the ammunition she had at her disposal and she could only pray it would be enough to make Roarke consign her to oblivion and go on to his next conquest.

The odds were in her favor, she argued valiantly as she climbed into her small compact and drove out of the parking lot. Kelley's ego was his vulnerable point. She'd

compared him to another man and found him severely
lacking in all areas. With any luck he would believe that
she had absolutely no intention of letting herself be se-
duced away from her husband. If he didn't choose to
believe her, then she would have to fight that battle
later. Today she had done all that she could. It was a
waiting game now.

But the fierce bravado that had fueled her resolve up
until that point faltered badly as she pulled into the
driveway of her new home and saw Gray's Mercedes
already parked ahead of her.

*Gray was home early.*

For an instant Amber froze behind the wheel. She
managed to turn off the ignition and set the brake, but
she couldn't seem to find the courage to open the car
door. He was bound to ask her where she'd been. The
thought of having to make up excuses for her absence
was enough to make her want to turn around and drive
back to the mall.

She could say she had been shopping. But she hadn't
bought anything. And it would be a lie. She had promised Gray that, while she might not answer all his
questions, she would never lie to him. It was only fair,
she knew, because Gray would never lie to her. Frantically she tried to put together some kind of coherent
answer that would satisfy his natural queries without
forcing her to tell the truth or a lie. Both seemed equally
bad alternatives at the moment.

It occurred to Amber that trying to handle Roarke
Kelley on her own might have been a very big mistake.

Even as that thought flashed into her brain, she saw
the front door open. Gray stepped out and walked toward the car. She knew as soon as she saw the calm, intent, implacable expression on his face that she wasn't

going to get out of this with a slick answer that gave nothing away. She'd seen this particular look on his face before, usually when he was dealing with a nasty business problem.

Amber sucked in her breath and finally found the strength to open the car door. If she'd been in a more cheerful state of mind, she might have discovered the whole situation reminded her of a Twitchell poem— something about gunslingers confronting each other on an empty street and knowing that only one would survive.

# 8

"MY MEETING WITH HARRISON was canceled." Gray offered the explanation for his unexpected return without any preamble. It was obvious he expected the same from her. He kissed Amber briefly, not seeming to notice her tense response.

"I see." Amber couldn't think of anything else to say as she walked back toward the house with him.

"I didn't know you had plans to go out this afternoon."

This was the point where she should just casually say she had decided to go shopping on the spur of the moment. Amber mentally tried the words out in two or three different variations and finally abandoned the whole idea of trying to finesse the situation. Gray was not the sort of·man you finessed. "I hadn't planned to go out. Something came up." She jammed her hands into her pockets and stalked into the house. Behind her she heard the door close with a sound of soft finality.

"You're upset," Gray said quietly.

Amber kept moving across the room until she was standing in front of the window. "Well?" she challenged, staring out at the lake. "Aren't you going to interrogate me? Ask me where I've been? What I've been doing?"

"Should I?"

She didn't hear him move, but his voice came from directly behind her. Amber could feel the solidity of him. It enveloped her and dominated the room. Her brief flare of defiance faded. Wryly she asked, "I don't suppose you'd be willing to assume I've just been out shopping and let things go at that, would you?"

"Have you been out shopping?"

"No."

"Then maybe you'd better tell me what you have been doing," Gray suggested calmly.

Nervously Amber yanked her hands out of her pockets and crossed her arms under her breasts. "Are you going to be that kind of husband, Gray?"

"What kind?"

"The sort who feels he has to keep track of every move his wife makes. Who grills her every time she leaves the house without permission. Who demands explanations for even the briefest absences."

A thread of amusement was laced through his words when he answered her. "I'll admit I'm possessive, but I'm not crazy. I think you know that, Amber. If I'm asking for some answers today, it's because I know something's wrong. It's been wrong since last night when you and your sister had that little chat outside by the car."

Amber sighed and surrendered to the inevitable. She turned around to meet his intent, waiting gaze. "I'm sorry, Gray. I wanted to keep you out of this."

"What is 'this'?"

"Old business," she told him with a grimace. "Embarrassing old business. I thought I could handle it on my own and with any luck I have."

"That's what you were doing today? Handling it on your own?"

She nodded and sank into a nearby chair. Stretching her jeaned legs out in front of her, she rested her arms along the sides of the chair and leaned her head back against the cushion. Morosely she looked up at Gray. "You asked me once what had happened in Southern California."

"And you didn't answer." He paced slowly across the room and took a chair by the window. Gray appeared totally relaxed, but there was a hard gleam in his eyes.

"I didn't answer because it was my past, and as far as I was concerned it didn't affect us."

"Now it does?"

She exhaled slowly, trying to find the words. "No. I think I've handled it. But I obviously didn't manage to handle it quietly enough to keep you from worrying, did I?"

"I'd worry about anything that upset you as much as this business seems to have done."

She smiled gently. "Thank you, Gray."

"Don't thank me. Just tell me what's going on."

Amber nodded. "It's not very complicated really. As you've guessed, I was involved with a man down in Southern California. I thought I was irrevocably in love with him. He was a race car driver, and the ad firm for which I worked had some contracts with him. He did various promotions for one of our clients. I got the account and therefore wound up working with Roarke Kelley."

Gray lifted one brow thoughtfully. "I've heard of him."

"You've probably seen him on TV advertising motor oil," Amber said grimly. "That man can sure sell motor oil. Or anything else, for that matter."

"Including himself?"

Amber frowned. "It doesn't matter. The upshot of the whole deal is that our relationship was traumatic, exciting, eventful and rather brief. It left me feeling as though I'd been through an emotional wringer. When it was over I knew I had to get as far away as possible. I quit my job and came here to Washington to look for a new one. I decided to take some temporary secretary assignments to make ends meet until I lined up something else. Then you hired me, and you know the rest."

"Uh-huh." Gray sounded remarkably noncommittal.

"Everything seemed to be working out just fine until last night when my sister told me Roarke was in town looking for me. It seems he was in an accident a couple of months ago and has had some time to think while recovering. He told Cynthia he wanted to see me again. She informed him I was married and wouldn't give him my new address, but she was afraid he'd discover it on his own, which he did. This morning he phoned and demanded to meet me. Said he'd show up on my doorstep if I didn't agree to see him one last time. He gave me his word that if I would just meet him and assure him that there was no hope for him and me and that I hadn't married you on the rebound, he would get back out of my life."

"What's his word worth, Amber?"

Amber's back teeth closed together as a brief flare of annoyance interfered with her noble determination to make a clean breast of the situation. She didn't care for the new tone in Gray's voice. "In point of fact, I don't think Roarke's word is worth much off the track. But I also know he has a rather massive ego. I made it very clear I wasn't interested in resuming our old relationship and that I was quite content with my marriage."

"Content?" Gray tasted the word curiously.

Exasperated, Amber lifted her eyes beseechingly toward heaven and wondered why everyone, her sister, Roarke and now Gray, kept stumbling over the word. "Yes, *content*. Happy, satisfied, committed. I am not looking for an affair, nor am I interested in relighting old flames. I met Roarke at the mall and made that quite plain to him. I told him to stay out of my life." Amber paused and then added meaningfully, "I was hoping that would be the end of things."

"The mall? You met him at the downtown shopping mall?" Gray looked unexpectedly amused.

Amber frowned. "Well, where else should I have met him? At a motel?"

The amusement that had lit his eyes faded at once. "You shouldn't have agreed to meet him anywhere."

Her jaw set stubbornly. "I didn't want him showing up here. That's what he threatened, Gray. The last thing I wanted was to have to deal with some sort of unpleasant scene between a new husband and an old boyfriend."

"I doubt that he'd have carried things that far. Very few men are that stupid. When you're out to steal a woman away from her husband, you work covertly. Subtly. You sneak around. You don't show up on the husband's doorstep and risk getting your face smashed in. He bluffed you with the threat, and you apparently fell for it."

Amber stared at him. "I know Roarke. You don't. I don't think it was a threat. It's the kind of thing he'd do. Roarke Kelley would be quite certain he could handle any mere husband. Knowing Kelley's penchant for drama, he'd probably enjoy causing such a scene. His reputation thrived on that sort of thing."

Gray studied her for a moment and then said gently, "Don't worry about it, Amber. If he shows up I'll take care of the matter."

Her mouth tightened. "I've already handled it."

"Have you?"

"Yes, damn it, I have. Stop looking at me like that, Gray. I'm a grown woman, perfectly capable of dealing with old problems from my past."

"You're a married woman. That means you've got a husband to help you deal with any old problems that arise." The inflection of Gray's soft, deep voice didn't change, but his next words were quietly underlined with steel. "You won't see him alone again, will you, Amber?"

She lowered her lashes to conceal both the surprise and the resentment that flared to life within her as she absorbed the implications of the coolly given order. Gray had phrased those last words as a question, but there was no doubt they were meant as a command.

Her surprise stemmed largely from the realization that in the three months she had been with him, Gray had never commanded her to do anything, not even type a letter. When it came to business, they worked together as a team; there was no need for orders. Amber simply did what needed to be done, following Gray's suggestions when she was involved in something new or difficult. In their private life he was equally easygoing and polite. He had always treated her with respect and consideration. Friendship underlay every element of their relationship. Friends did not give orders to each other.

As far as Amber was concerned, she didn't approve of husbands giving orders to wives, either. But she was willing to acknowledge that a husband who found himself in a situation such as Gray had just experienced might believe he had reason to be somewhat concerned. She tapped one fingertip on the arm of the chair.

"I have no intention of seeing Roarke again," Amber finally said diplomatically. She refused to directly acknowledge Gray's quiet command, but she didn't mind admitting that the last thing she wanted to do was see Roarke Kelley again.

Gray's eyes flicked briefly to the tapping finger and then went back to her face. He nodded once, as if satisfied with her somewhat oblique response to his equally oblique order.

Amber had the odd sensation that her new marriage had just traversed a somewhat sticky spot. She wasn't quite sure how to interpret the event, but she sensed that on some level something had changed. It had to do with the fact that she was accepting Gray's right to occasionally indulge the possessive side of his nature. Beyond that she didn't want to explore too thoroughly. Instinctively she knew that acknowledging such basic factors as masculine possessiveness and husbandly rights added a new and more volatile dimension to a marriage that was supposed to be founded on friendship and quiet contentment.

"What exactly did Kelley say to you, Amber?"

Her eyebrows came together impatiently. "Not much."

Gray smiled fleetingly. "You can't blame me for being curious."

Her frown deepened. "I don't see the point in rehashing the whole conversation. It's over. I told him I was married and intended to stay that way."

"Did he ask you to go away with him?"

"The conversation didn't get that far!" Amber snapped resentfully. "For heaven's sake, Gray, I told him I wasn't interested in him and that was the end of it."

"How did you convince him that you weren't interested in him?"

Amber's uncertain mood was about to explode in a rare burst of feminine temper. "Roarke's as egotistical as they come. He's also highly competitive. Hardly surprising since he makes his living in such a competitive sport. I hit him at his most vulnerable spot by drawing up a quick list of points that compared him to you and made it clear he was a noncontender."

Gray winced. "Uh-oh."

Amber glared at him. "What do you mean by that?"

"Your strategy might not have been the best, honey. You said yourself he's highly competitive. Making him look like a loser was probably not the best approach under the circumstances."

"Nonsense," she retorted. "I know what I'm doing."

"Is that right?" Gray looked faintly amused. "In what way did you compare the two of us?"

Amber flushed, remembering. "It's not important."

"Maybe not, but I'd like to know."

Temper and tension came together, and the resulting explosion left Amber with almost no control over her tongue. She came up out of the chair in a restless surge of energy and stalked to the window. "All right, if you must know, I told him that he was weak while you were strong, that his sense of honor was open to question while yours was solid gold and that, while he was good-looking, you were the kind of lover for whom a woman would willingly commit murder. There. Satisfied? That was the essence of the whole conversation. I got up and left him sitting alone with his cup of coffee. The entire meeting didn't last more than fifteen minutes, and it took place in full view of everyone in the mall who happened to be strolling past the café."

She sensed rather than heard him move. Amber didn't turn around as she felt the comforting large shape of him directly behind her. Then his blunt, wonderfully sensitive fingers lightly touched the curve of her throat. Instantly the resentment and tension faded. She wanted nothing more than to let herself sink into the tender strength of Gray's arms. It had been a very trying day.

"Tell me again," Gray murmured, "about how good a lover I am. Would you really commit murder to get into my bed?"

Amber pivoted and found herself folded in his arms. "Egotist," she grumbled happily against his chest. A vast sense of relief welled up inside her.

He laughed softly and kissed the top of her head. His hands moved deliberately down the length of her back. "What did you expect after telling me that? I have a strong urge to maintain my status on your list."

"Right now?"

"Right now. One of the advantages of working out of one's own home. Come away from the windows, my love. I don't want to share you with some jerk in a boat who has a pair of field glasses." He drew her back from the panoramic view and then stopped to explore the nape of her neck with his lips. Amber shivered with pleasure, and Gray felt the reaction instantly. "I love the way you catch fire when I touch you. I can't get enough of it."

Neither could she, Amber realized with a sense of wonder. She was indeed quite content in her marriage. At the moment she didn't want to think beyond that single word. Everyone else might find it a curious description of her feelings, but she was satisfied with it. When Gray's fingers found the hem of her gold sweater and lifted it over her head together with the camisole she wore underneath, she closed her eyes in pleasure.

Using a rapidly developing sense of touch, Amber began to unbutton Gray's shirt and unbuckle the belt of his slacks. They undressed each other with growing hunger, and when their clothing was scattered in an untidy heap on the floor, Gray pulled Amber down onto the leather couch.

She landed in a sensual sprawl on top of him, thoroughly enjoying the freedom of movement the position gave her. The warm excitement in her eyes made Gray laugh huskily.

"What's so funny?" she demanded, punishing him lightly with her teeth.

"Some day I'll tell you," he promised. His fingers slid along her spine and paused to draw slow, compelling circles at the sensitive point of her lower back.

Amber arched like a sleek cat, wanting to demand a more complete answer to her question but too consumed with desire to insist on one. Gray could occasionally be quietly, but firmly stubborn. Besides, there were more interesting things to do at the moment. She splayed her fingers on his chest, enjoying the feel of him. "I think I like being on top."

"I've noticed. There's an assertive streak in you, lady." His eyes gleamed. He trailed his fingers a few inches farther, tracing the curve of her buttocks until Amber gasped and wriggled against him.

She could feel the full shaft of his manhood stirring against her lower body, and the knowledge that she had such an immediate and powerful effect on him pleased her enormously. She moved again, this time with sensual deliberation, and was rewarded by a low groan deep in Gray's chest.

Slowly she used her flattened palms to push herself up until she was sitting astride Gray's strong thighs. Watching him through half-lowered lashes, she stroked her fingertips down his body until she was touching him intimately, teasingly, tantalizingly.

"Sweetheart, you're playing with fire."

"I know."

"You'd better be prepared to douse the flames." He fit his hands to her hips, lifting her easily until she was positioned just above him.

"Any time," she promised. Amber felt the first probing touch of him against her, and her nails sank convulsively into the muscles of his chest. Then the probe became a fierce, blunt pressure that made her tighten with excitement. "Ah, Gray," she whispered thickly as he lowered her slowly downward until he was buried in her.

She took charge then, delighted in being able to set the pace. Gray seemed content to let her until the last few moments when his own passion threatened to erupt.

"Now, sweetheart," he urged roughly, the gold in his eyes very intense.

"Are you sure?" She couldn't resist teasing him, even though the tightening coil of sexual tension in her lower body was about to snap.

"I'm sure." His fingers clenched into her thighs.

"Soon," she murmured, slowing the pace just enough to frustrate him.

"I can't wait any longer."

"Yes, you can." She slowed the rhythm a bit more and then cried out softly as his fingers tightened in response.

"I think I've had about all I can stand of your brand of teasing, honey."

"Is that a threat?"

His laugh was very low and very sexy. "You bet your sweet tail it is."

He moved then, lifting her, sliding out from under her and pinning her beneath him in one swift, powerful motion that made Amber's senses spin. She moaned with excitement and pleasure as he parted her legs and again surged into her. Her head went back over his arm, her eyes tightly shut and her hair fanning out around her in a soft tangle.

"Wrap your legs around me," Gray ordered, his voice taut with passion. He kissed the tip of her breast as she willingly obeyed. "That's it. My God, you drive me crazy."

"Oh, Gray, I can't wait any longer." Now it was Amber who was pleading for release. She strained against him, seeking to force him more deeply into her hot, damp warmth. Her breath came in quick, pulsing beats.

"Soon," he said, pulling back slightly.

"No, *now*."

"You can wait."

"I can't possibly wait. If you don't finish this, I'll fall apart."

"You'll fall apart, anyway. You always do in my arms. I'm getting addicted to the response I get from you." He tormented her further by again withdrawing until he was just barely inside her.

"*Gray*, please...?" She didn't know whether to laugh or cry or scold. She was delirious with desire. A fire was consuming every nerve ending in her body, and she knew she had to quench it or go mad with frustration.

"You're not the only one who can tease." But his own face was a mask of barely checked passion. It was all Gray could do to draw out the suspense even a few more seconds.

"You're not teasing me, you're torturing me!"

"Never," he assured her with a gently mocking sensuality that made her nip at him with her sharp little teeth. "Ouch!"

"Do your husbandly duty or I'll take another bite," she vowed.

"I shouldn't surrender to threats. It sets a bad precedent."

"But you will surrender, won't you?" she pleaded softly as she tightened her legs around his waist and lifted herself once more.

"Oh, God, yes," he groaned and let slip the last of his control. He poured himself into her, sheathing himself to the hilt in the snug velvet channel.

Amber sucked in her breath and then she was whispering Gray's name over and over again in a litany of release and satisfaction. Her own name mingled with his as Gray groaned and shuddered heavily against her. The climax caught them both and whirled them through the frenzied rapids of release and into the quieter waters of relaxation that followed.

For a long time Amber lay beneath Gray's heavy, utterly replete body and gazed dreamily up at the ceiling. Her fingers drifted in lazy, languid patterns on his back as she thought about the man who held her now and the man who had thought he could seduce her this afternoon.

The list of comparisons she had drawn up on the spur of the moment to convince Roarke that he didn't stand a chance was only the beginning, Amber realized. She could have gone on and on making such comparisons, and Roarke would have fallen short on every point. It was hard to imagine how she could once have been so captivated by Kelley. She had been a fool, little knowing what had waited for her in the future. If she had, she wouldn't have wasted so much emotion on a good-looking race car driver whose only real assets were the ability to drive a car and sell motor oil.

Then again, Amber thought with sudden insight, perhaps she wouldn't have been able to appreciate what Gray had to offer if she hadn't been through that traumatizing experience with Roarke. Life had a way of teaching its lessons very thoroughly. Impulsively she put her arms around Gray and hugged him.

He reluctantly lifted his head and looked down at her, a smile playing at the edge of his mouth. "What's that all about?"

"Nothing, I'm just happy."

"Content?"

She smiled, not noticing the watchful, appraising gleam in his eyes as he studied her. "Very."

THE NEW ISSUE of *Radiant Sunsets* arrived the next morning. Amber found it immediately in the pile of mail she had retrieved from the mailbox and raced back into the house waving the small journal triumphantly.

"It's here! Ms Abercrombie's article is here. I'm going to read it first. I can't wait to see what she had to say."

Gray lounged back in his swivel chair and groaned. "You might as well read it aloud. I want to see just how nutty Honoria Tyler Abercrombie really is."

Amber grinned and sat down in her own chair, tossing the remainder of the mail carelessly on the desk. Eagerly she opened the little journal to the table of contents. "Here it is, 'The Use of Erotic Metaphors in the Poetry of S. U. Twitchell.' Page twenty-three."

"I'm getting incensed already."

"I haven't even started," Amber assured him with relish.

He cocked one brow. "*You* haven't even started?"

"I meant I haven't even started to read it."

"Oh. Well, don't keep me in suspense."

Amber began to read the article in a grave tone. The piece was every bit as serious as any of the ones Gray had written. Ms Abercrombie cited the same poems Gray had referenced in his last article, drawing entirely different conclusions. The piece concluded on page twenty-five, and Amber finished reading it with barely repressed jubilation:

"It is obvious from the above examples of Twitchell's art that he was not simply a balladeer or a teller of legends. His goal was far more complex and sophisticated. The subtle, erotic quality he brings to such poems as 'The Ballad of Billy Ballantine' and 'Gunslinger's Lament' are not isolated examples. His poetry is infused with similar sexual metaphors.

"Twitchell was clearly obsessed with ways of equating guns with manhood. The weapons of the Old West are classic phallic symbols in his work. But in this respect he simply shares in the ubiquitous male mystique perpetrated by later chroniclers of the West.

"S. U. Twitchell's unique quality was in taking the erotic references much farther than other Western poets have done. He doesn't limit himself to using guns as sexual metaphors. No, indeed, Twitchell goes beyond that. He uses practically every landscape description, everyday Western artifact and every heroic confrontation in a metaphoric sense. Each line is laced with sex.

"In Cormick Grayson's recent article, 'The Desert as a Metaphor for Psychic Isolation,' the author completely misses the point of the poems cited. Grayson appears totally oblivious to the fact that Twitchell is actually using the barren landscape as a symbol of the female's rejection, of course, which fuels the lonely quests of the gunslingers and cowboys who populate Twitchell's poetry. One can only speculate upon the sort of traumatic rejection Twitchell himself must have at some time received at the hands of a woman, but it is clear that it influenced all his work.

"The cowboys and gunmen described by S.U.T. are doomed to be forever proving their manhood with a gun, presumably because they can't do it in any other way. One can only assume that Twitchell himself had a few problems with his own sexuality. I find it fascinating to speculate on why Mr. Grayson has chosen to overlook this aspect of Twitchell's work."

As Amber read the last lines of the article, Gray exploded out of his chair and stalked toward the window. He was seething with righteous indignation.

"The woman is obviously a repressed nitwit who can't even read poetry properly," he informed Amber grimly. "Of all the idiotic, ridiculous conclusions. Sexual metaphors in Twitchell? Hah! That's absolute garbage."

Amber kept her expression one of thoughtful speculation. "I don't know about that, Gray. I can certainly see Ms Abercrombie's point about the references to iron. And now that I think about it, it's possible to view several other things in his work as possible sexual metaphors."

"That's pure bull." Gray swung around and paced back to his chair.

"Why?" Amber inquired innocently.

"Why? I'll tell you why. Because Sherborne Ulysses Twitchell was such a lousy poet he couldn't possibly have figured out how to use guns or anything else as sexual metaphors. I doubt if Twitchell even knew what the term 'metaphor' meant." He slouched back in his chair and dared Amber to contradict the conclusion.

"Hmmm. A very telling argument," she was forced to agree. "Twitchell really was a terrible poet. No sense of rhyme, rhythm or meter. Not much ear for the language, either."

"See what I mean?" Gray was triumphant now. He smiled with dangerous certainty. "Abercrombie will be sorry she ever set pen to paper. I'm going to write a rebuttal immediately."

"What about the Symington report?"

"It can wait another day or two. Putting Honoria Tyler Abercrombie in her place is far more important."

"I don't see how you can complain about Ms Abercrombie's views on metaphors in Twitchell's work. After all, that last article you wrote claimed he was using the desert as a metaphor for loneliness. If he was capable of using one kind of metaphor, he was capable of using another," Amber stated.

"Don't be silly, Amber. I made all that up about Twitchell's use of the desert as a metaphor for loneliness."

Amber's eyes widened. "You did? Good heavens, Gray, in that case you really can't complain about Ms Abercrombie's inventing a few things about his work, either."

"Oh, yes, I can," he retorted bluntly. "I'm the authority on S. U. Twitchell. It's my prerogative to make up anything I want about him. But I'll be damned if I'll let Honoria Tyler Abercrombie have the same privilege. I'm going to blast her off the printed page."

"I'm sure she'll be quite terrorized."

"I don't know," Gray said thoughtfully. "I have a feeling the woman's tough. Convincing her to give up and surrender might take some doing."

"Is that what you want from Ms Abercrombie?" Amber asked curiously. "Surrender?"

Gray's eyes narrowed. "Unequivocal capitulation. Nothing less will do."

Amber was startled. "Good grief. I had no idea you were so serious about all this."

"You still have a few things to learn about me, Amber," he explained almost gently.

She paused reflectively before picking up the rest of the mail. She was thinking about the way he had quietly laid down the law on the subject of Roarke Kelley and the passionate way he had made love to her afterward. "I'm beginning to see that."

# 9

THE CALL FROM the used bookstore came the next day shortly after Gray had left for the rescheduled Harrison meeting. Amber was delighted with the shop owner's report, and she dialed her sister's number a minute after she'd assured the shopkeeper she would be picking up the book that afternoon.

"Amber, I was just going to call you," Cynthia said as soon as she heard her sister's voice. "I've been dying to know what happened between you and Roarke. Did he find you? Has he called?"

"It's a short and uninteresting story, but if you want to drive over to Seattle with me this afternoon I'll tell you the whole sordid tale."

"Sounds good. I'll leave Drake with Mrs. Benson. Why are we going to Seattle?"

"Because a bookstore over there has at last found a copy of a volume that may or may not have been authored by one Sherborne Ulysses Twitchell at the peak of his creative power."

"Twitchell's peaks were lower than some of the valleys of other poets," Cynthia observed. "Did Gray order the book?"

"No, I did. It's going to be a surprise for him. He doesn't know anything about it."

"You sound excited."

"I am. Gray's going to get a charge out of this. He'll be all on fire to prove the authorship of the volume."

"Amazing what it takes to set that man on fire. Pick me up in half an hour. I've got to run. Drake's opening his mouth in a very threatening manner." Cynthia hung up the phone just as Drake started squalling in the background about something that had offended his two-year-old sensibilities.

Amber replaced her own receiver with a rueful smile. She had been around Drake frequently enough to know it didn't take much to offend him. Cynthia had her hands full. Glancing down at the notepad in front of her, Amber reread the title she had jotted down a few minutes ago when she was talking to the shopkeeper. *Cactus and Guns: A Collection of Western Ballads*. The author was listed on the title page as Anonymous. Good old Anonymous, Amber thought with a grin. The poems in this collection must be so bad even Twitchell wouldn't claim them.

"I don't get it," Cynthia said forty minutes later as Amber guided her compact onto the long floating bridge that crossed Lake Washington. "How did you find out about this book in the first place?"

"A couple of months ago Gray was working on an article for one of those little newsletters he writes for, *Poets of the Southwest*, I think, and he came across a reference to this book. Someone had quoted a short poem from it in one of the little poetry journals and had listed the author as anonymous. Gray said it sounded amazingly like a Twitchell poem."

"That bad?"

"Yeah." Amber laughed. "That bad. Ultimately he decided it couldn't be Twitchell, but I wasn't so sure so

I put in a standing order at the bookstore for it. The owner promised to keep an eye out, and sure enough she called today."

"How much is this little surprise going to set you back?"

Amber shrugged. "Not much. Ten dollars or so, I imagine. If I hadn't shown some interest in it, I'd probably have gotten it for a quarter. Anything that looks or sounds like Twitchell isn't likely to command a great sum. How's Drake?"

"Hale and hearty. It's a relief to get away from him for an afternoon, though. I love him dearly, but to tell you the truth, I'm looking forward to going back to work soon."

"With any luck you'll be able to go back to your old job at the bank."

"Speaking of employers . . ."

"What about them?" Amber was through the tunnel at the end of the bridge and heading toward downtown Seattle.

"Are you going to be sticking with yours?"

Startled by the question, Amber slanted her sister a quick glance. "What's that supposed to mean? Of course I'm sticking with Gray. Why shouldn't I?"

"You're his wife now. Doesn't that make working for him a little awkward?"

"Not in the least. Nothing's changed."

Cynthia was unconvinced. "I don't know. I can't imagine working for Sam. I'm passionately in love with the man, and I'm afraid the emotional side of our relationship would be apt to interfere with the business side."

"That's not a problem for Gray and me," Amber assured her with full confidence. "We've been working together successfully for over three months. Nothing's changed since our marriage."

"Nothing?"

"Nope. He was always one of the world's more relaxed and lenient employers," Amber said with a quick laugh.

"Yes, I know, but he's also your husband now."

"It doesn't make any difference. Professionally he treats me the same as he always has. He respects me. Makes me feel like an equal in the business. It's like a partnership."

"But he's still the senior partner," Cynthia reminded her bluntly.

"Well, yes, I suppose so. But the fact hardly gets in our way. What are you driving at, Cyn?"

"I'm not sure," her sister replied honestly. "I'm just trying to figure out how things work between you and Gray. When you first went to work for him, I was sure it would be just a temporary assignment. You've got to admit, your typing isn't all that great."

"Gray figured that out right away," Amber confessed. "I've had a lot of experience putting together ad campaigns for motor oil and windshield wipers but very little practice typing. But I'm passable. I got two whole reports out for Gray before he realized I wasn't the fastest typewriter jockey in the world. By then he'd decided I had other qualities."

"You mean he loves you for your brain?"

For some reason Cynthia's teasing question made Amber vaguely uneasy. "I mean he respects my business abilities and has a use for them in his consulting work."

"Come to think of it, you were rather good with his clients the night of the party. They seemed to take to you and Gray made sure they all met you."

"If advertising taught me nothing else, it taught me how to get along with difficult clients," Amber agreed wryly. "What's this all about, Cyn?"

"I told you. I'm curious. There's something rather fascinating about your relationship with Gray. I can't quite figure it out."

Amber shrugged as she turned the car down Fourth Avenue. "There's nothing to figure out. We're friends, business associates who work well together and we're also husband and wife."

"And you're content with your marriage," Cynthia concluded.

Amber made a face. "What is it with that word that makes everyone look at me in such a strange way?"

Cynthia ignored her. "Tell me something, were you still content with your marriage after you saw Roarke?"

"Believe me, seeing Roarke again made me realize what a good decision I made when I accepted Gray's proposal," Amber said with great depth of feeling. "That bastard."

"Roarke?"

"Of course, Roarke. I would hardly refer to Gray that way. Roarke was out to cause trouble. I think he just wanted to see if he could work the old Kelley charm again. I gather he has some spare time to kill before he's ready to go back to racing. He thought he'd kill it with me."

"I take it the effort wasn't successful?"

Amber shook her head. "Not a bit. I told him to pack up and leave the vicinity. I never wanted to see him again."

"You told him you were, uh, content with your marriage?"

"Damn right I did. And I meant it. I made sure he knew it."

"Where did you meet him?"

Amber pulled into a parking garage, paused to take the ticket from the automatic dispenser and started the car up the winding path to the next floor of parked cars. "At the mall."

"The mall? Good Lord. How odd."

"What's odd about it?" Amber asked in exasperation. She remembered the brief amusement that had lit Gray's eyes when she'd told him the same thing. "Where was I supposed to meet him?"

"I don't know." Cynthia said, chuckling. "I guess I didn't consider the problem. Poor Roarke. A man like that can't be accustomed to having women arrange to meet him in busy shopping malls. So unromantic."

"I didn't want to meet him at all," Amber said in a low tone as she parked the car. "He threatened to come out to the house if I didn't."

Cynthia grimaced, her voice reflecting total feminine understanding of the situation. "What a mess that would have been."

"Yes."

"Still, it would have been interesting to see how Gray would have handled such a scene. He's so calm and placid and easygoing."

Amber closed her mouth and opened her car door without saying a word.

"Amber?" Cynthia climbed out and stood frowning at her over the roof of the compact. There was dawning chagrin in her eyes. "What is it, Amber? Gray doesn't know about Roarke, does he? You said you met Roarke at the mall."

"I did." Amber collected her bag and started purposefully toward the exit.

"But Gray found out? Amber, what happened?"

"Gray was waiting for me when I got home from the mall. His meeting was canceled."

"What meeting? Oh, I see. He'd been at a meeting when you arranged to see Roarke. So he got back home ahead of you?"

"Yeah."

"Well? Was that such a big deal? You just said you were at the mall doing a little shopping, didn't you?"

Amber sighed, wishing she'd never gotten involved in the conversation. "Gray isn't the sort of man you lie to or even try to finesse for that matter. He's very astute."

"Oh, my God."

"Don't sound so horrified. It was hardly a major event. I told him about Roarke and that I was perfectly capable of handling my past on my own."

"How did he take it?"

"Quite calmly. How else would Gray take anything? Cynthia, he and I are *friends*. Friends respond in a calm, rational way to incidents such as Roarke's appearance."

"Still . . ." Cynthia hesitated. "Didn't he say anything, well, *unfriendly* or irrational at all about the situation?"

Amber was feeling pressured now. "No, he did not. He simply advised me not to see Roarke on my own again."

"Advised you?" Cynthia's voice sounded suspiciously weak.

"That's right."

Cynthia cleared her throat. "Wasn't he at all firm on the subject?"

"I've had about enough of this ridiculous conversation," Amber stated firmly. She didn't want to think about those few moments during the interview with Gray when she'd sensed the steel that lay beneath the surface calm of the man. It had been an awkward little scene, but both she and Gray had put it behind them. Roarke Kelley had not been mentioned since. "I've told you the whole story. Let's talk about something else."

"What an amazing man," Cynthia said. She sounded bewildered.

"Yes, he is, isn't he?" Amber knew she sounded distinctly complacent. She smiled to herself and led the way out of the garage and down the street to the bookstore that had uncovered the precious copy of *Cactus and Guns*. Cynthia followed quickly.

Inside the store Amber introduced herself pleasantly. The bookstore owner, a rounded, beaming woman in her early fifties, produced the prized volume with a flourish.

"I don't believe I've ever had a call for this particular book in my entire career in the business," the shopkeeper said politely as she handed the huge, heavy, leather-bound volume to her customer.

Amber stared at the brass-trimmed corners and the tooled leather binding with a sense of mild shock.

"Good heavens. I had no idea it would be so heavy." The book was nearly a foot high and must have weighed several pounds.

"All handmade," the shopkeeper assured her. "You don't find leather bindings like that anymore."

"No, you certainly don't," Cynthia agreed with a chuckle.

"It's illustrated, you know," the woman behind the counter went on encouragingly as she realized her client was still rather taken aback by the size of the book. "Take a look inside. Lovely little pen-and-ink sketches."

Eagerly Amber turned the heavy pages. "Why so it is. Cynthia, if it turns out that Twitchell did the sketches as well as the poems, this will be an absolute gold mine. It will add a whole new dimension to Twitchell. Artist as well as poet." She studied a small picture of a saloon on a busy Western street. The sense of perspective was slightly off, and the drawing was rather vague.

"Who's going to be able to tell if he did the sketches?"

Amber grinned. "We'll leave the authentication up to the world's foremost Twitchell scholar. But since this drawing is almost as bad as the poetry, I don't think there can be much doubt. Gray's going to have a great time with this. Whole new realms of Twitchell studies will be opened. Listen to this:

And Billy rode for justice;
Yes, Billy rode for honor.
Billy rode for Texas,
Where he met up with Big Jack Bonner.

Oh, they'll sing of Billy's guts.
They'll sing of Billy's glory.

They'll sing tall tales of Billy.
Till every cowboy knows his story."

"What perfectly amazing poetry," Cynthia said deadpan. "Who was Billy, or shouldn't I ask?"

"His full name was Billy Ballantine. He was a gunslinger who was always coming up against other gunslingers who wanted to challenge him. Big Jack Bonner was one of the meanest. The poem is called 'The Ballad of Billy Ballantine,' and the fact that it's in this book is highly significant. It's a good indication that S.U.T. actually was the anonymous author. That poem also appears in the *Collected Works*."

"You sound very knowledgeable on the subject," the shopkeeper observed.

Amber smiled brilliantly. "My husband is an authority on Twitchell."

"I see." The older woman returned the smile. "You're pleased with the book then? It's what you wanted?"

"I'm thrilled. How much do I owe you?"

The volume turned out to be considerably more expensive that Amber had estimated, but as they walked away from the shop she strongly defended the purchase to her sister.

"It'll be worth every penny just to see the look on Gray's face when he opens this book. If this isn't Twitchell's work, it's bound to be a deliberate imitation. That alone would be fascinating."

"Why?" Cynthia demanded as they headed downhill toward the waterfront.

"Because Twitchell is such a bad poet that it's highly unlikely anyone would want to deliberately imitate him. The fact that someone might actually have done so is mind-boggling," Amber explained.

Cynthia shook her head. "I don't think I'm ever going to understand the literary mind."

"Me, neither." Amber tapped the paper-bound package under her arm. "But, then, I've never actually met a literary mind."

Both women burst out laughing. By mutual consent they had decided to have lunch at one of the sidewalk fish counters on the waterfront. They collected bowls of chowder and two large containers of steamed clams from one of the busy vendors and found seats in a sitting area that was shielded from the brisk November weather. From their vantage point they could sip chowder and watch the busy Elliott Bay shipping traffic. The day was crystal clear, and the snow-covered peaks of the Olympic Mountains formed a stunning backdrop to the picturesque setting.

"Tell me something, Amber," Cynthia began in a confidential tone, "and I want the truth. Just what, do you think, is the appeal of Sherborne Ulysses Twitchell for Gray?"

Amber surprised herself and her sister by taking the question seriously. "Well, he has great fun with Twitchell of course. . . ."

"I know that, but there must be something more."

"He *is* the world's only known authority on Twitchell," Amber reminded her. "Unless you count Honoria Tyler Abercrombie."

"Who?"

"Never mind." Amber took another spoonful of chowder and stared thoughtfully at a ferry that had just left the terminal and was heading for one of the islands that could be seen in the distance. "I think Gray likes Twitchell because, in spite of the fact that the guy was a lousy poet, there's a fundamental slice of the Old West in his work. The *mythical* Old West. You know what I mean, the one that we all respond to on some level. Good guys versus bad guys. Self-reliance. Justice. The importance of the land. Nearly everything Twitchell wrote had to do with that old Code of the West. His gunslingers and cowboys and marshals are always world-weary, and they're loners but honorable in their own way. The good guys always do what has to be done. They look after themselves and the people who depend on them. They ensure that justice gets done and that innocent people are kept safe even if they have to handle things themselves without the aid of the institutionalized forces of law and order."

"Something in all that appeals to Gray?" Cynthia asked perceptively.

Amber nodded. "I think so. I believe that if he'd lived a hundred years ago he would have come West and taken his chances on the frontier. There's something in him that reminds me of the characters in Twitchell's poems."

"Well, thank goodness he doesn't wear a gun strapped to his thigh," Cynthia said forcefully, but her eyes were full of a new understanding.

Amber shuddered. "Yes, thank goodness for that. A little of the Code of the West goes a long way—" She broke off suddenly as she caught sight of a familiar dark head. "But speaking of good guys versus bad guys . . ."

"Amber, what is it?" Cynthia glanced over her shoulder and saw Roarke Kelley making his way purposefully toward them. "Oh, no. It's Kelley."

"He must have followed us." Amber was furious. "That bastard. What does he think he's going to accomplish by hounding me this way?" She began wadding up the paper napkins and plates from which she had been eating. "Come on, Cyn, let's get out of here."

Amber and Cynthia were on their feet by the time Roarke reached their table. He smiled his slow, boyish smile and nodded pleasantly toward Cynthia. "What a surprise to run into the two of you."

"Yes, isn't it." Amber scowled at him. "If this particular sort of coincidence keeps happening, I'm going to report you to the cops, Roarke. There are laws against harassment in this state."

"Harassment?" He looked deeply offended.

"It would be a little embarrassing to have charges filed against you, wouldn't it?" Amber pointed out too gently. "Bad for your reputation as a racetrack Romeo."

"I'll take care of my own reputation," he promised meaningfully. His blue eyes were glinting with amusement. "There's no need to run from me, honey. All I want to do is talk."

Amber didn't respond. She was getting nervous. She ignored Roarke and glanced at her sister. "Ready, Cyn?"

"I'm ready." Cynthia had obviously decided to follow Amber's lead. She smiled vaguely at Roarke and stepped around him. "Excuse me, please."

Roarke's amusement faded. "Amber!"

Amber didn't look back. She dumped her crumpled trash in a nearby container and kept moving. Cynthia hurried to follow.

"You can't keep running, Amber, and you know it," Roarke called after her.

Amber was striding briskly along the sidewalk now with Cynthia in her wake. "Damn him," she muttered furiously. "Maybe Gray was right."

"Right about what?" Cynthia glanced back once, as if curious.

"Right about me not trying to handle Roarke alone."

"Hmmm." Cynthia appeared thoughtful. "Maybe he was. Kelley is turning out to be persistent, isn't he?"

"He doesn't know what it means to lose," Amber explained. "I think Roarke's always gotten everything he ever wanted."

"And now he wants you?"

Amber grimaced. "If he does, it's only because he's been told he can't have me. If I dropped everything and ran back to him, I'd soon find myself in the same position I was in back in California."

"And you wouldn't want that because you've decided you prefer quiet contentment to flaming passion and the feeling of being head-over-heels in love, right?"

For some reason her sister's half-amused comment irritated Amber. "Right," she agreed firmly. "I also prefer being married to a man I can trust. One who doesn't fool around with other women while swearing he loves me. One who knows the meaning of the word commitment."

Roarke didn't follow the two women as they made their way quickly back to the parking garage. Amber drove home with a feeling of anxiety that wouldn't dissipate. She knew she wasn't really worried about Roarke Kelley. It was Gray's reaction when she told him what had happened that concerned her. She was quite innocent of course. The meeting today had hardly been her fault. But she was afraid Gray wasn't going to be at all happy. A part of her was worrying that the man with whom she had established such a satisfactory, friendly, egalitarian marriage wasn't going to prove quite as understanding as he should be on this particular subject.

GRAY LEFT THE LOBBY of the gleaming high rise that housed the offices of Harrison's firm and started toward the parking lot where he had left the Mercedes. He was looking forward to getting home, taking off his tie and jacket and settling in for the evening with his wife. The pleasant domestic routine of a drink before dinner, helping Amber in the kitchen and chatting about everything from world events to S. U. Twitchell's role in the literary universe had become thoroughly addictive, just as Gray had suspected. He thoroughly enjoyed being married to Amber.

He was pleased with life these days. His world was very nearly complete, and it was the first time he could ever remember it being that way. But, then, he hadn't fully realized what he'd been missing until Amber Langley had knocked on his front door slightly over three months ago. Amber Langley Grayson now, he reminded himself with a feeling of deep, possessive satisfaction. His wife.

She was his, although she hadn't fully accepted the fact. He knew she preferred not to think about their relationship in elemental terms. Right now she was in the process of becoming accustomed to the role of wife and lover. Apparently she preferred to do so without questioning her own emotions or his too closely. She still needed a little more time. Some of the barriers were still there, but they were crumbling rapidly. Amber had given him almost everything, although she hadn't quite realized it yet. When she did realize and accept it, Gray's world would be perfect and complete.

There was no rush, he told himself as he walked between two parked cars. He was a patient man.

He was contemplating his own patience when he sensed the change in the atmosphere behind him. Automatically Gray kept moving forward until he was free of the confines of the two parked cars. Then he sidestepped quickly, swinging around to confront whatever it was that had disturbed old instincts and triggered half-buried alarms. Somehow he wasn't greatly surprised to see Roger and Ozzie closing in behind him. They paused when they realized he had become aware of their presence.

"Good afternoon, boys," Gray said calmly. "No offense, but you look a little out of place here." They were probably freezing in those lightweight nylon windbreakers, he thought. Underneath the jackets, he suspected they had on only the short-sleeved resort-style shirts they had favored in Tucson. Jeans and running shoes completed their outfits. The clothing wasn't much defense against the chill November air. They scowled at Gray and kept their hands shoved into the pockets of their windbreakers.

"Mr. Delaney sent us to talk to you again," Roger growled.

"Yeah, well, I figured you probably wouldn't come all this way to visit me on your own." Gray waited, absently cradling the leather case full of business papers under his arm.

"You haven't turned in your report to Symington yet, according to Mr. Delaney. Mr. Delaney wants to make it real clear that the Symington deal has to go through."

"Then Mr. Delaney should be discussing the matter with Symington. I'm not thinking of buying that resort, Symington is."

"Delaney says Symington will do whatever you say," Ozzie muttered.

"He's wrong. Symington makes his own decisions. I'm only the consultant. Now, if you'll excuse me, boys, I've got work to do."

"Sorry, Grayson." Roger didn't sound sorry at all. The truth was, his voice was chilled with a new sense of anticipation. "It's not going to be that simple."

"It is for me," Gray informed him. "Look, kids, you already tried the bribe and the threat of a little rough stuff. Neither worked, so why don't you just pack it in and go home?"

Ozzie swore viciously. "Don't call me a kid!"

"Sorry." It was Gray's turn not to sound particularly sorry. "But that's how you're acting, like kids. A couple of young punks who don't know what it means to play in the big leagues. Take some advice and stay out of this game. You'll last longer if you stick to your own weight. Delaney must have been desperate to try to use you two."

Roger moved forward a couple of steps, his handsome face twisted with anger. "You're wrong, you know. We only tried the bribe. We never did get around to trying the rough stuff. That wife of yours faked us out with the bodyguard act."

Gray's mouth curved wryly. "The fact that she did it so easily proves my point. You both bought her act hook, line and sinker until it was too late. It was really very funny. Was your boss amused?"

"So amused he decided we should take the act on the road and maybe make a few changes in it," Ozzie said deliberately.

Gray didn't say anything. He just looked at Ozzie and smiled.

"You think we're joking, don't you?" Ozzie said between his teeth.

"No, I think you're stupid."

"You want to hear about the changes in this little road show? I don't think you're gonna like 'em. There are some major differences this time around. The little lady isn't going to get to play bodyguard. In fact, her part of the act has been completely rewritten. Mr. Delaney thinks you might be a lot more understanding about his position if we try the rough stuff on her."

Gray didn't move, but the cold, alert state of awareness that had been filling him since he'd realized he was being followed was suddenly a thousand times more intense. The expression on his face didn't change, but the sardonic quality in his eyes became quietly, immeasurably more dangerous. Neither Roger nor Ozzie seemed to notice, or if they did they simply didn't comprehend what had happened.

"The two of you have overstayed your welcome. I suggest you go back to Tucson and practice your golf." Gray turned away and walked the rest of the distance to the Mercedes without bothering to glance back. He would know if they decided to rush him. Roger and Ozzie were very easy to read.

But they didn't make a move, and Gray slipped into the car without further incident. They had disappeared from sight by the time he had the Mercedes headed out of the parking lot. Gray drove home with a grimly thoughtful expression. Handling Roger and Ozzie wasn't going to be the problem.

The problem was how to handle Amber.

He couldn't tell her the truth. She wouldn't understand what he was going to do. She didn't know much about people like Roger and Ozzie, and Gray had a hunch she would flatly refuse to be sent out of town for a few days if she suspected he was planning to deal with the Tucson Twins on his own.

She would insist on calling the police, not realizing how little the cops could do until a crime had been committed. She would be horrified at the thought of Gray taking matters into his own hands. What's more, her passionately protective instincts would make her refuse to be sent out of harm's way. She would stand by him come hell or high water, just as she had that night outside the resort in Tucson. And the last thing Gray wanted was for her to be anywhere in the vicinity when he took care of Roger and Ozzie. Given her bold nature, she might very well get hurt. The thought was intolerable.

No, all things considered, there was no alternative. Amber had to leave town for a few days and that meant he had to find a way to make her go without letting her know why she was being sent away.

Gray had a hunch he was in for the first real argument he'd had with his wife. She probably hadn't realized how close they had come to one the other day when they had "discussed" Roarke Kelley, he thought wryly.

*Roarke Kelley*. Gray repeated the name to himself, and his hands tightened briefly on the steering wheel.

Kelley was the answer. Gray knew he had the reasonable excuse he needed for playing the heavy-handed husband.

# 10

AMBER WAS CURLED UP in a chair in front of the wide expanse of windows that lined the living room when she heard the Mercedes turn into the drive. She didn't look up. She was still studying what she had just written on the front flyleaf of the large volume she had purchased that afternoon.

She had sat down with a pen in her hand intending to write a witty little inscription to Gray. She had toyed with the notion of a short imitation verse that would sound like Twitchell. Two or three possible couplets had formed in her head. But instead she had set pen to paper and written something entirely on impulse, something very different from what she had planned to write. Now she just sat staring at the words and wondered why it had taken her so long to recognize the truth.

When the front door opened she was jerked out of her reverie. Hurriedly she closed the book and stuffed it back into the paper bag. She set it on an end table just as Gray came into the front room.

Amber looked up with a welcoming smile that faded slightly as she sensed the unfamiliar hardness radiating from him. Slowly she uncoiled from the chair, her eyes questioning. Quickly she went toward him, stood on tiptoe and brushed her lips against his in greeting.

His mouth stayed hard beneath hers. "Gray? Is something wrong?"

"It depends on your point of view." He shrugged out of his jacket. "Pour me a drink, Amber. Pour yourself one, too. We're both going to need it." He walked away down the hall toward the bedroom.

"Gray!" Genuinely worried now Amber hurried after him. "For Pete's sake, tell me what's wrong!"

He was standing in front of the mirror unbuttoning his shirt. His eyes met hers in the reflective surface, and Amber went cold.

"We're going to have a small talk about Roarke Kelley," Gray said quietly.

Amber felt the blood leave her face. She was stunned. In that moment only one thing was clear to her. *He knew she'd seen Roarke that day.*

All her notions of being involved in a gentle alliance between friends went up in smoke. She'd never seen Gray in this mood, but she had to admit she'd had hints of this steel in him the day he'd told her she wasn't to meet Kelley alone again. Her mouth went dry. "You want to talk about Roarke? Gray, how did you know? I mean, how could you possibly have guessed? I was going to tell you about what happened today. Honestly I was. I wasn't keeping secrets. You just walked in the door. I haven't even had a chance to explain."

He swung around, his eyes narrowing. If she hadn't known better, Amber could have sworn he looked surprised for a brief instant. But that wasn't possible because he obviously already knew about her seeing Roarke today. After all, what other reason was there for him to bring up the subject again?

The odd expression in his gaze vanished, and the cool steel returned. "All right, I'm listening. Explain."

Flustered now, Amber struggled to regain her sense of self-control. Her ridiculous reaction to Gray's grim mood was unsettling. She was exasperated both with herself and with him. She was also undeniably nervous. Her palms were damp with the evidence of her anxiety. Unconsciously she dried them on the fabric of her jeans, unaware that Gray was watching with a deep, speculative interest.

"There's not much to tell." Amber lifted her shoulders helplessly. "Cynthia and I went into Seattle today to do some shopping and we had lunch on the waterfront. Roarke showed up during lunch. We left immediately. End of story." She frowned. "I can't see how you knew about it. But I assure you I had no intention of keeping it secret."

"Didn't you?" He stood there with his shirt unbuttoned, his hands on his hips and his feet slightly braced. His eyes were enigmatic.

"Of course not. But I still don't see how—" She broke off staring at him in shock. "Roarke didn't contact you, did he? Has he . . . has he said anything? Implied anything? If he has, you can be sure it's nothing but lies. I give you my word of honor that nothing happened today and I didn't encourage him in any way." She took a deep breath and said in a surprisingly steady voice, "Tell me what's going on, Gray."

"Nothing I can't handle. Alone."

Her eyes widened. "What's that supposed to mean?"

Gray regarded her intently for a long moment and then stripped off his shirt and walked to the closet to pull out a casual dark pullover sweater. The strong muscles of his shoulders rippled easily with the movement. "I want you out of town for a few days, Amber."

"Out of town!" She was so startled she couldn't find anything else to say.

"I'm going to send you to Vancouver for the rest of the week."

"Vancouver?" This was getting crazier by the minute. All she seemed to be able to do was echo his own words. "Vancouver, Canada?"

"That's right. I've got friends up there. Mitch and Lacey Evans. I've mentioned them. You'll stay with them." He had the sweater on now and was facing her once more.

Amber was staring at him, openmouthed with shock. "You're sending me up to Canada? To get me away from Roarke? I don't believe it. Gray, I assure you, you're overreacting. This isn't like you. What on earth did Roarke say to make you threaten this sort of thing?"

"I'm not threatening anything," he told her quietly. "I'm simply going to put you on the plane to Vancouver this evening. You'd better go pack. Mitch and Lacey will meet you at the airport."

Amber finally managed to fight her way through the fog of unreality that was on the verge of swamping her brain. For the first time anger came to her aid. She drew herself up proudly and confronted her husband. "Your friends can go to the airport if that's what they feel like doing, but I'm not going to be on the plane and that's final. You are not sending me out of town simply because Roarke Kelley is telling lies. Cynthia was with me this afternoon when we ran into Roarke. You can ask her what happened. I will not stand here and be accused of . . . of infidelity on the basis of the word of a man like Kelley. I've told you his word isn't worth much!"

"I'm not accusing you of anything. I'm simply taking precautions. Go pack, Amber." There was a quiet command in his voice that was utterly shattering. "I'm going to call Mitch."

Amber stared at him as if she'd never seen him before. This wasn't the man she had come to know in the past three months. This was a stranger who was actually beginning to frighten her. "I won't let you do this to me, Gray. I won't let you do it to *us*."

"We'll be leaving for the airport in fifteen minutes." He stepped past her, heading for the telephone in the office.

"Gray, please, listen to me."

The desperation in her words finally seemed to get through to him. He paused halfway down the hall in the doorway of the office. For a moment Amber felt a brief, flickering sense of hope that was soon extinguished. The slight softening of his eyes must have been an illusion.

"We'll talk about it when you return from Vancouver. I give you my word, Amber. But right now I want you out of town. I'll handle this on my own."

"Be reasonable," she pleaded. "What good will it do to send me away?"

"You'll be out of Kelley's reach."

"Has he threatened to run off with me? That's idiotic. I wouldn't go!"

"I'm not taking any chances. As your husband I have a responsibility to take care of you. I'm doing what I think is best under the circumstances. You'll have to trust me."

He disappeared into the office leaving Amber to stare after him. Her mind was churning with pain and panic. She couldn't seem to think straight. The sense of un-reality was overwhelming now. None of this could be happening. Not to her and Gray. She wasn't an errant wife to be packed off to some distant location because she was threatening a scandal. And Gray was not a heavy-handed, domineering husband who saw him-self as his wife's lord and master. None of this made any sense.

Amber was still telling herself the same thing much later that evening when she got off the plane in Van-couver. She was dazed and must have looked it. The couple who came forward to greet her had concerned expressions on their faces.

"Amber Grayson?" The woman, who was about Amber's age, was small and petite, her short blond hair done in a stylish flounce that framed wide, intelligent eyes. "I'm Lacey Evans and this is my husband, Mitch. Gray asked us to meet you."

"How do you do," Amber replied woodenly. Mitch was a few years older than his wife and had started to put on a little weight around the middle. It didn't soften the blunt lines of his tanned face, however. His hair was dark brown and his eyes were a curious shade of green. He was smiling at her, but there was something in his eyes that reminded her briefly of Gray. There was no logical reason for the similarity. The men were not at all alike. Amber frowned at the impression and dis-missed it. She clutched her shoulder bag, aware of a terrible sense of awkwardness. These people must know why she was here.

It was humiliating. If she'd stopped to think just how embarrassing this situation would be, she would have found some way to avoid Mitch and Lacey. Instead, she'd walked off the plane like a dazed victim of combat and straight into the arms of the strangers Gray had sent to meet her. The truth was Gray had given her very little opportunity to think through the situation. Somehow he had taken control completely. She had been on her way to the airport before she'd had time to muster any real resistance. For the first time she wondered what kind of friendship Gray had with Mitch Evans that could be imposed on to this extent.

"You must be hungry," Lacey was saying with a determined cheerfulness. "It's only a short hop from Seattle, and they don't serve much on board the plane, do they? We usually drive between Seattle and Vancouver. We're going out to dinner in town, unless you have any objections. There's a wonderful new Indian restaurant that Mitch and I have been wanting to try. Having a guest gives us a great excuse."

"Is this all your baggage?" Mitch said, hoisting the carryon Amber had been holding.

"Yes, that's it. There wasn't much time to pack and I...I don't expect to be here long." Amber heard the lost quality in her own voice and mentally gave herself a fierce shake. She had to pull herself together. She was acting like an idiot.

But Mitch seemed unaware of her dazed condition. His green eyes flickered over her with unconcealed curiosity. "No, I don't imagine you'll be here long at all. Gray will take care of things in his usual style, and you'll be safely on your way back home very soon.

Came as a real surprise to hear he was married. It's about time."

Lacey grinned at Amber. "We'd begun to think he'd never get around to finding the right woman. But we should have known better. Gray always does things in his own time and in his own way, but they do seem to get done, eh?"

Amber nodded, bleakly aware that she couldn't think of anything to say. She was too busy coping with the knowledge that Mitch and Lacey Evans seemed to know all about her and the reason she was here. Embarrassment was Amber's dominant emotion at the moment. It blanketed even the anger that was simmering deep inside her.

Neither of her hosts made any reference to Roarke Kelley as they drove into the city. They both kept up a lively conversation as if sensing Amber wasn't yet able to hold up her end of things. Amber was oblivious to the spectacular array of lights that in the daytime would give way to an even more spectacular view of mountains and sea. The city of Vancouver was framed in a setting of natural grandeur that almost never failed to impress. Under normal circumstances, Amber was as susceptible to the beauty of the scenery as every other visitor. But tonight did not constitute a normal set of circumstances.

She sat in the back seat of the car and nominally tried to pay attention to the friendly strangers chatting in the front seat. But her mind was still churning with questions that had no answers and fears that couldn't seem to focus.

By the time Mitch had found a parking spot downtown and led the way into the beautifully decorated

Indian restaurant, Amber was finally beginning to pull herself together. She realized for the first time that Gray had given her no chance to think or react in a logical manner. He had simply issued his orders, made it clear he expected total compliance and then swept her off to the airport where he'd made certain she'd boarded the plane. Amber had never before witnessed that particular side of his nature. It had thrown her for a loss. Coolly and deliberately, Gray had taken full advantage of her confusion.

Seated at a table across from Mitch and Lacey, Amber opened the elaborate menu and eyed the selection of tandoori dishes, curries and distinctive breads. Forcing herself to choose a meal was the first attempt she had made in the past few hours to concentrate her thoughts on a single point. The exercise proved useful. When she set down her menu, she was able to meet Mitch and Lacey's perceptive gazes for the first time.

"I assume you both know exactly why I've been thrust on you like this?" she began politely.

Mitch didn't answer. His green eyes were thoughtful. It was Lacey who leaned forward with a gently understanding, sympathetic expression. "You're not to worry about a thing. Gray told Mitch all about that horrible Kelley person who's been bothering you. He's going to take care of everything and in the meantime you're very welcome here. Gray is an old friend of Mitch's, you know. Mitch would do just about anything for him."

"Is that right?" Amber assimilated that bit of news. "How long have you known my husband, Mitch?"

"Years," Mitch said easily. "Gray and I worked together a few years back. We were a team."

"You're a U.S. citizen?"

"That's right. I came here on a visit after I quit my job. I met Lacey here. She's Canadian, as you can tell if you listen to the accent, eh?" Lacey shot him a spirited look of protest as he gently mocked the lilting "eh" that ended many of her sentences. "After that, there wasn't much point in moving back over the border." He smiled at his wife. "We have a condo out in the West End near Stanley Park. Lots of room, so don't worry about imposing. With any luck maybe Gray will join us for a few days after he's handled things down in Bellevue."

"There is nothing down there for Gray to handle," Amber said pointedly. "Except his overactive imagination."

Lacey blinked in surprise. "I don't understand."

"Neither do I," Amber said thoughtfully. "And the more I think about it, the less I understand it. He must know that Kelley is no threat to our marriage."

Mitch eyed her. "Why shouldn't he worry about the guy? I'd sure as hell worry if some ex-boyfriend of Lacey's took to hanging around her."

"A husband and wife should trust each other," Amber said sadly. "I thought Gray trusted me."

Lacey bit her lip. "I'm sure Gray doesn't mean for you to think he lacks trust. He's simply trying to protect you."

"From Roarke Kelley? That's ridiculous. I'm hardly likely to run off with the man. I'm married to Gray, and I'm completely committed to the marriage. He knows that. Or at least I thought he knew it."

Mitch looked distinctly uncomfortable. "I'm sure this doesn't have anything to do with a lack of trust," he said gruffly. "Gray just wanted you safely out of the way while he deals with the matter."

"I'd like to know exactly what Gray thinks he can do to Roarke," Amber muttered.

"Don't worry about Gray. He knows what he's doing," Mitch assured her, more cheerful now, as though he felt on safer ground. "He always did have a way of knowing what he was doing. That man has the patience and the perseverance of the devil or a saint. I was never sure which. Occasionally he has the same kind of luck, too."

"He doesn't need any of those things to deal with Roarke Kelley," Amber said darkly. "All he has to do is ignore Roarke, the same as I was doing."

NEARLY TWO HUNDRED MILES AWAY in Bellevue, Gray paced through the house and thought about how lonely it seemed now without Amber. He walked from room to room, aware of the deep hunter's patience that had settled on him. There was no need to go looking for his quarry. Roger and Ozzie would come to him, if not tonight then tomorrow night at the latest. Neither of the young toughs would be able to wait much longer than that. Gray would be ready. The moment they stepped over his threshold, they would be taking one step too far. They would be well and truly into the trap.

In the kitchen he made himself a cup of tea and then he wandered back out into the living room. His gaze fell on the paper-wrapped parcel lying on an end table. Idly he went forward to investigate. It must have been something Amber had bought this afternoon in Seattle.

He unwrapped the package and found himself looking at a heavy brass-trimmed volume. Immediately he was intrigued. Setting down his mug of tea, he opened the book and saw the inscription on the flyleaf. He stood gazing at it for a very long time and then, with great care, he carried the book over to the black sofa and sat down with it.

Some of the patience in him gave way before a sense of great eagerness. He wanted Amber back where she belonged as quickly as possible.

But first he had to handle Roger and Ozzie.

As A CONNOISSEUR of such places, Cynthia would no doubt have loved the huge underground shopping mall, Amber thought wryly as she obediently plowed along behind Lacey Evans. Under normal circumstances, Amber had to admit, she herself would have had fun exploring the collection of small shops and large department stores that formed the maze in downtown Vancouver. But it was impossible to take any pleasure in today's shopping trip, although Amber was doing her best to hide that fact. Two phone calls last night had proven to Amber just how abnormal the situation really was. She was no longer just angry with Gray. She was worried about him.

The first call had been frustrating. Mitch and Lacey had insisted on phoning Gray after dinner to let him know that Amber had arrived safe and sound and was settling in nicely. Mitch had dialed the number, but after a few jovial comments he'd abruptly handed the receiver to Amber. There hadn't been much else she could do except get on the line.

"Everything okay, Amber?" Gray had asked gently.

"I want to come home."

"Soon. I promise. Do you like Mitch and Lacey? They're nice people."

"I want to come home."

Gray had sighed. "I know. I'll come up there and get you in a few days."

"You don't seem to be listening, Gray." Amber had been fiercely aware of Mitch and Lacey trying not to listen. They had taken themselves off to the kitchen. Staring at the lights of Vancouver outside of the high-rise condo window, Amber had said, "I'm hurt and I'm angry and I want to come home."

There had been a pause on the other end of the line. "You want to come home even though you're hurt and angry?"

"I want to come home so that I can wring your neck." Amber had not waited for a response. She'd quietly slammed down the receiver. When Mitch and Lacey had wandered cautiously back into the living room, she'd greeted them with her most brilliant smile—the one that fairly radiated high-voltage charm. "Gray assures me everything is under control and I'm to have a good time."

Mitch and Lacey had appeared quite relieved at her obvious change of mood. For the rest of the evening Amber had made it clear that she was going to enjoy her short stay in Vancouver. She had become the quintessentially charming houseguest. By the time she had finally gone to bed, Lacey had made plans for taking her shopping the next day.

The second phone call had been made hours later. If Amber hadn't still been lying wide awake staring at the lights outside the bedroom window, she would never have heard Mitch Evans pad quietly down the hall and dial the number.

At first she had assumed he was merely going to the kitchen for a glass of water. But something about the nearly silent way he had moved had alarmed her. If the floor outside her door hadn't squeaked faintly, she probably wouldn't have heard him at all. She had lain still for a moment or two trying to figure out just why his passage had disturbed her. Then it had come to her. Mitch had moved with the same near-silent tread that characterized Gray's footsteps. She had remembered how her first impression of Mitch's watchful green gaze had also put her in mind of her husband.

Without giving herself more time to think, Amber had tossed back the down comforter and had slipped into her robe. She had intended to have a chat with Mitch Evans. If Gray wouldn't give her answers, perhaps she could talk his friend into doing so.

But the answers had begun to come the moment she had opened her bedroom door. She was able to hear the low murmur of Mitch's voice on the telephone in the living room. Moving cautiously so as not to make the floor squeak the way Mitch had, Amber slipped out into the hall. By the time she was nearly as far as the living room, she was able to hear Mitch's side of the conversation quite clearly.

"She's settling in just fine, Gray. Stop worrying about her. Lacey's going to take her shopping tomorrow.... Yeah, I know. She was still simmering when she got off the plane, but by the time we were halfway through dinner she'd relaxed and accepted the situation.... Of course I'm sure. Lacey agrees with me." Mitch gave a small chuckle. "Too bad you used the ex-boyfriend as the reason for shipping her off to us. Lacey says any woman would be humiliated by being treated like a disgraced wife.... I know you didn't have much choice. Your options were limited. You could hardly tell her about the two strong-arms from Tucson, could you? That would have really panicked her. This way she's just mad, not scared."

Amber sucked in her breath, her whole body going tense as she stood barefoot in the hall and listened to the rest of the conversation. The strong-arms from Tucson. Roger and Ozzie were involved in this. That explained everything. Apparently Vic Delaney hadn't given up his notion of trying to convince Gray to lie to Symington. Gray hadn't dared tell her the real reason he'd wanted her out of town. He hadn't wanted her to worry, so he'd ensured she got angry instead.

Idiot male. Functioning under the old Code of the West, no doubt. Get the womenfolk safely out of town while the lone marshal confronts the bad guys in the showdown in front of the saloon. Except this wasn't a case of the good guys versus the bad guys; this was *one* good guy confronting *two* bad guys. Not the best odds. The last time this had happened Amber had been the one to handle the situation. It was infuriating that Gray could have forgotten so easily. She stopped mentally rehearsing what she would say to her husband the next time she saw him and concentrated on listening to the remainder of Mitch's conversation.

"Look, I know you can handle this, Gray, but are you sure you don't want some backup? Okay, but if you change your mind, let me know. I can be down there in less than four hours by car. Even faster if I can get a convenient flight. Be like old times, wouldn't it?" There was a pause. "Yeah, I agree. Sounds like a couple of amateurs. Watch yourself, though. The trouble with amateurs is that they behave like amateurs. How the hell did you ever get yourself into this situation? I thought the consulting business was as safe and cozy as the engineering field." There was a low chuckle, and Mitch began to wind up the conversation.

Amber had quickly retreated down the hall to her bedroom where she'd spend a good portion of the rest of the night awake. Her mind had been spinning with questions and answers. By the time she had finally fallen asleep, she had decided on a plan of action.

The next day she had drummed up the same degree of exuberant enthusiasm for Lacey's proposed shopping trip as she would have done for a new ad campaign. At breakfast both Mitch and Lacey had seemed to buy the image. Mitch had left for the downtown office of his engineering firm after a final perusing glance at Amber's animated features. He'd seemed satisfied. After he'd gone, Lacey had innocently outlined the activities she'd planned for the rest of the day.

Thus far Amber had been treated to a tour of the fascinating little shops that lined Robsonstrasse, scones and tea at one of the quaint cafés nearby and finally this trip through the largest of the underground malls. It was nearly four-thirty. Soon Lacey would suggest they leave for home. She and her husband planned to take Amber to a Japanese restaurant tonight.

"I want to go back to Eaton's and have another look at that dress," Amber said as she accompanied Lacey into a small boutique. "Why don't I meet you at the bookstore upstairs?"

"I'll come with you," Lacey had exclaimed quickly.

"There's no need. It's getting late. Go ahead and finish your shopping here and I'll meet you in the bookstore just before five." Amber smiled with innocent reassurance. It was her "You can't go wrong with this ad" smile.

Lacey again bought the image. She returned the smile and walked on into the shop. Amber immediately headed up the escalator to the sidewalk outside where she quickly found a cab. With any luck Mitch and Lacey would soon find the note she had left behind on her bed before Lacey had taken her shopping.

Half an hour later Amber was headed south to Washington in a rental car. It would take her about four hours to get home.

SHORTLY AFTER SIX THAT EVENING Gray was surprised by the ringing of the telephone. He put down the heavy volume of *Cactus and Guns* and reached for the receiver. Even before he heard the self-disgust in Mitch's voice, he knew something was wrong.

"You're going to have my head for this, pal," Mitch began unhappily. "I lost her."

Gray gripped the phone so tightly it was in danger of cracking. "What the hell are you talking about, Mitch?" His voice was far too soft, and Mitch knew it. His friend sighed.

"She went shopping with Lacey this afternoon and disappeared inside one of the malls. Lacey waited for her at the rendezvous point until five-thirty and then finally decided Amber had taken off. When she got home there was a note on Amber's bed. She says she's had enough of playing disgraced wife. She's headed for California."

"California!" Gray sat on the edge of the sofa staring blankly at the night-darkened view through the windows. *California.*

"You want me to come down there so you can pound me into the ground in person, or shall I just stay here and drink poison?" Mitch asked.

"You're sure she left for California?"

"That's what her note said. She was very upset, Gray. More upset than Lacey and I had realized, I'm afraid. She covered it beautifully."

Gray closed his eyes briefly. She had been hurt and angry and she wanted to come home so that she could wring his neck. Instead she'd left for California.

"Gray?"

"Forget it, Mitch. There's nothing you can do now. I have a hunch I'll have things settled down here this evening. Then I'll start looking for Amber."

"If she's on her way to California, she should be safe enough for the next twenty-four hours while you clean up that little consulting mess." Mitch was trying to look on the positive side.

"Yeah."

"I'm sorry as hell about this, Gray. Five years of the soft life can change a man. In the old days I wouldn't have bought that great smile of hers for a minute."

"She sold a lot of ad campaigns with that smile. No reason you shouldn't be as susceptible as any other client. Stop blaming yourself, Mitch. As you said, she should be safe enough for now. Tell Lacey not to feel guilty. My wife has a mind of her own."

"When this is over bring her up here and we'll try another visit. This time we'll make it the four of us instead of the three of us."

"I'll do that. Good night, Mitch."

Gray replaced the receiver and remained sitting on the sofa staring out the windows. It was going to be a long night.

Shortly before ten he heard a car in the drive. Gray was on his feet immediately. The brief burst of exultant relief was quickly submerged beneath a layer of deep foreboding. Amber hadn't gone to California after all.

He leaped for the door, praying his luck would hold long enough for him to get her safely into the house. But even as he wrenched open the door his instincts told him he was too late.

Amber was climbing out of the car. She was moving very slowly and carefully because Roger was standing in front of her on the drive. He was holding a gun. Ozzie was right beside him.

As light from the hall spilled out onto the drive, Roger and Ozzie and Amber all turned their heads toward the man filling the doorway.

"We're going to give you one more chance to write that report to Symington just the way Mr. Delaney wants it written," Roger told Gray. He motioned Amber forward with the gun. "This time I think we may have found a real convincing argument."

# 11

AMBER FELT DISORIENTED as she walked slowly toward the open door. She was vividly aware of the gun in Roger's hand as he moved behind her. The moment she'd turned off the key in the ignition Roger and Ozzie had stepped out of the bushes that lined the drive. She knew she'd walked into the middle of the showdown Gray had apparently anticipated.

"Hello, Amber," Gray said calmly as she came through the door. His eyes were unreadable. "Are you all right?"

She clutched the strap of her purse, ignoring the two young hoods behind her as her eyes clung to Gray's. "I'm fine."

"You're an hour late."

"The traffic out of Vancouver was worse than I'd expected." She couldn't believe they were having this seemingly casual conversation. It was one more indicator of her sense of disorientation.

"Step back, Grayson," Roger ordered as Ozzie shut the door. "You, too, lady. Let's all go into the living room and make ourselves comfortable. You got here just in time," he added to Amber. "Ozzie and I were just thinking about inviting ourselves inside for a chat with your husband. We'd been waiting for just the right moment. Didn't know his clever little bodyguard was about to drive up in a car. We thought you were already inside snuggled in for the night."

Amber didn't need to look at Gray's expression to know that he'd planned her departure very carefully yesterday. He'd even managed to get her out of town without letting Roger and Ozzie know she was gone. Of course she'd spoiled the plans by returning unannounced. She imagined Gray would have a few things to say on that subject later. Well, it was his own fault, she told herself ruthlessly. He should have known better than to try to send her away at a time like this.

"Don't worry about these two, honey," Gray was saying quietly. He reached out and took her hand, tugging her gently back toward the sofa. "They're just a couple of amateurs."

Amber stared at the gun in Roger's fist and decided she was just as glad there didn't seem to be any "professionals" in the vicinity. Amateurs were quite bad enough. She was grateful for the strength in Gray's hand.

"Amateurs, Grayson?" Ozzie's eyes were a little too bright, almost feverish in intensity. "Is that what you think we are? You don't know what the hell you're talking about. You're the amateur. Thought you could ignore Mr. Delaney's request and get away with it."

"And after Mr. Delaney was so nice to you and your wife down in Tucson." Roger shook his head sadly. "Ingratitude. That's your whole problem, Grayson. Ingratitude. The least you could do to make amends is write a real good report to Symington. Better make sure you give it your best shot, because if the deal doesn't go through, Mr. Delaney is going to send us back to finish what we're supposed to start tonight."

Amber shuddered. "You've delivered your warning. Now get out."

Ozzie chuckled. "There's more to this warning than a few polite words, Mrs. Grayson. We've already tried words with your husband. He's the stubborn type. We're going to have to give him a little demonstration. Show him we mean business, if you know what I mean."

Roger nosed up the barrel of his handgun. "You're going to help us make our point, Mrs. Grayson."

Amber stared at him in disbelief. It was Gray who responded, his tone still infinitely calm. No, Amber decided, it was more than merely calm. There was a frighteningly fathomless element in his words. Listening to him was like standing in the depths of a lost cavern and looking over the edge of a bottomless pit.

"She's got nothing to do with this," Gray said. "This is between Delaney and myself. Let her go."

"Now, Grayson, you don't really expect us to do that, do you?" Roger grinned evilly. "We already told you that this time around we'd be using your wife to get our point across."

"You don't need her to do that."

Amber listened to the exchange with sudden comprehension. Roger and Ozzie had threatened to hurt her. No wonder Gray had ordered her to pack yesterday and then shoved her onto an airplane and sent her off to stay with friends.

"I think we do need her," Ozzie stated, staring at Amber's still face. "Besides, we owe her a little something for that trick down in Tucson. Come here, lady."

Amber didn't move. "Go to hell," she said, her voice almost as calm as Gray's. She felt his fingers tighten briefly around her hand and then he released her.

"I said, come here!" Ozzie reached for her. "We're going to work you over a little and let your husband watch. Bound to make him feel more like writing a real positive report to Symington."

"You'd better tie him up, first," Roger advised as Amber stepped hastily out of reach. He indicated Gray, who was standing with his back to the sofa immediately behind him. "We don't want him trying to play hero."

"My pleasure." Ozzie took a length of wire out of his pocket and began untwisting it. "Put your hands behind your back, Grayson."

"What makes you think I'm going to make this easy for you?" Gray asked mildly, not moving.

"Grab the woman," Ozzie instructed his pal.

"I told you they were amateurs, Amber," Gray remarked as Ozzie moved forward with the wire. "Just a couple of small-timers. They're good at threatening to beat up a woman, but that's just about their limit. They're never going to make it in the big time. That's because they haven't got the guts to go up against a man."

"Shut up, Grayson," Roger hissed. He swung the gun back and forth between Amber and Gray. "Come over here," he snapped at Amber, who again didn't move. "I said get over here, damn you!"

"I'll take care of her just as soon as I finish tying him up," Ozzie promised. "But first I think I'm going to soften him up a little. Amateurs? Grayson, you don't know the meaning of the word. You're the amateur around here." He launched a short, punching jab that caught Gray in the chest.

Amber gasped as Gray sprawled down onto the sofa. "Gray!"

"Keep your mouth shut," Roger growled. He was watching avidly as his partner leaned down to haul his victim up off the sofa for another assault.

What happened next was a blur of motion that Amber had a hard time explaining later. Gray came up off the sofa just as Ozzie reached down to grab his arm. But he didn't come up empty-handed. The light glinted on the cold blue steel in his fist.

"What the hell . . . ? Roger, he's got a gun!" Ozzie scrambled backward, but he was too late.

Gray held the gun in his right hand and used his left to deliver a short, violent chop against the side of Ozzie's neck. Ozzie went down without a whimper. Roger yelled as he saw his partner fall to the floor. Instinctively he leaped to gain a shield. His hand snaked out to grasp Amber's wrist and pull her toward him.

But Amber already had her hands on the heavy brass- and leather-bound volume of *Cactus and Guns* that had been left lying on a sofa cushion. She swung wildly with it and felt the book collide jarringly with Roger's gun.

There was an explosion of sound that shattered one of the mirrors behind the couch, and Roger screamed in rage. His gun clattered to the floor. Amber scrambled out of the way, breathing quickly as she took in the situation. Her eyes flew to Gray.

"I've been telling you for over three months that there are times when there's nothing quite like a bit of

Twitchell's poetry." Gray spoke without taking his eyes off Roger.

"I see what you mean." Amber glanced at the heavy volume that had landed on the floor. "A real literary heavyweight."

"Are you okay, Amber?"

"Much better than I was a few minutes ago."

Ozzie moaned and stirred at Gray's feet. Gray stepped aside. "It would seem," Gray went on mildly, "that there's been a realignment of power here. Amber, pick up Roger's gun. We wouldn't want him getting any ideas."

Amber hurried over to where the weapon had fallen when she'd swung *Cactus and Guns*. She scooped up the gun, a little surprised by how heavy it was. "I've got it." *A big iron*, as Twitchell would have said.

"Good. Now call the police so that we can get these two out of here once and for all."

"We should have called the cops a long time ago," Amber muttered as she picked up the phone.

"We didn't have any real charges to bring against Roger and Ozzie until tonight, at least not strong enough charges to keep them out of our hair." Gray smiled briefly. "But now we do. They made all sorts of mistakes tonight. Like I said, amateurs."

Roger glared at him. Ozzie moaned again and lay still. Amber ignored them both and began dialing.

The sound of a car in the drive a few minutes later came almost at the same instant that Amber was hanging up the phone. "Good heavens, how did the cops get here so fast?"

"I doubt if it's the police. See who it is before you open the door, Amber. We've had enough houseguests this evening."

She didn't argue. Hurrying forward she put one eye to the small glass peephole in the front door just as the doorbell rang. "Oh, Lord," she said.

"Who is it?" Gray was still watching his captives, the gun held easily in his hand.

"You're not going to like this, Gray."

"I haven't liked much at all about this evening's events. Who is it?"

"Roarke."

"Ah." It was impossible to tell from his voice what Gray was thinking.

"I didn't invite him here!" Amber yelped, swinging around to plead her case. Of all the things to have happen, she thought in panic. This was really too much.

"Open the door."

"Open the door? Are you crazy, Gray? Why should I open the door?"

He flicked her a brief, half-amused glance. "Just do as I say, Amber. Open the door."

The bell sounded again, and Amber spun around, her hand on the knob. This was insane. She didn't know whether to be horrified or infuriated. She was very definitely outraged. She flung open the door to reveal Roarke Kelley lounging arrogantly against the frame.

"What are you doing here?" she flared furiously. "Nobody wants you hanging around here."

His mouth curved in a slow, knowing smile. "Are you sure about that, Amber? I think you want rescuing, and I'm here to do just that."

Her eyes widened as she tried to imagine how Roarke could possibly have known about the violent scene that had just taken place. "Rescuing?"

He grinned. "From a life of boring domesticity. I'm going to remind you of what it was like with me in the old days."

"You promised me you'd go away and stay away. Your word of honor can't be trusted any more now than it could be six months ago."

"You and I have things to talk about," he said in a low, sexy drawl. "Did you really think I'd let you send me away before we've solved our problems? I've been doing a little research on one Cormick Grayson. He's not your type at all, honey. Where is this dull, plodding, businessman husband of yours? I want to see the man you're using to hide behind."

For the first time that evening a spark of amusement lit Amber's eyes. She stepped back and gestured grandly toward the living room. "He's right over there. Why don't you come on in and meet him?"

Her answer was obviously not quite the response Roarke had been expecting. Nevertheless, he stepped into the hall and glanced into the living room. He came to an abrupt halt as he took in the grim tableau in front of him.

Gray spared him one cool, uncurious glance, his gun never wavering from his captives. The casually controlled way he held the weapon spoke volumes. "Hello, Kelley. How's the motor oil business these days?"

Roarke was clearly stunned. He must have decided he'd just walked into a homicide scene. Amber came up behind him feeling a strong sense of satisfaction as she realized just how frozen with shock Roarke actually was.

"What the hell is going on here?" Kelley croaked.

"These two men were bothering me," Amber explained smoothly. "They kept hanging around and making threats. But as you can see, Gray has taken care of them. I don't think they'll be giving us any more trouble."

"I don't like other men bothering my wife," Gray explained very politely. "I'm sure you can understand my feelings on the subject."

"My God!" Kelley backed up a pace, his eyes riveted on the gun in Gray's hand. "You're crazy," he whispered in a hoarse, strained voice. He swung around to face Amber, his expression a mask of astonishment and fear. "You're both crazy." He leaped for the door.

Amber got out of his way, turning to watch as Kelley slammed the door of his Porsche and violently revved the engine. Gravel spun under the tires as he backed hurriedly out of the drive. Even as the Porsche disappeared around a corner of the road, Amber could hear the police sirens in the distance.

"I thought you said he wouldn't have the unmitigated stupidity to actually show up on our doorstep," Amber complained over her shoulder to Gray as she watched the official cars pull into the drive.

"So he's dumber than I expected. Not my fault. Probably made one too many motor oil commercials. Rots the brain. Don't blame this on me. I thought you were convinced you'd sent him packing," Gray retorted.

Amber sighed. "Yes, well, I may have misjudged the situation slightly."

"It doesn't matter now," Gray assured her. "I have a hunch he won't be back."

Amber remembered the expression on Roarke's face as he shot out of the hall and raced for his car. Gray was right. Kelley wouldn't be back to bother her. She could just imagine what the little scene in the living room had looked like to him. He probably felt lucky to have escaped alive. She was grinning as the first policeman reached the front door.

SEVERAL HOURS LATER Amber was no longer smiling. She had assumed her most serious expression as she paced back and forth in front of the living room windows and lectured Gray in her sternest voice.

Gray was taking the lecture with his usual aplomb, but once or twice Amber had been convinced she'd caught a brief flicker of humor in his green-and-gold eyes. It only made her redouble her efforts to get across her point.

"You," she announced, leveling a pointed finger in his direction, "are going to answer a few pithy questions."

Gray exhaled slowly. "Yes, ma'am."

"Where did you get that gun?"

"I found it under the sofa cushions. Amazing what gets lost under furniture cushions. We'll have to tell the cleaning lady to be more careful in the future."

Amber halted and faced him with her hands on her hips, her brows drawn fiercely together. "Don't you dare get flippant with me, Cormick Grayson. I want some answers. Where did you get the gun?"

He eyed her intently for a moment and then said evenly, "I own it. I've had it for years. It's licensed, if that's what you're worrying about."

She threw up her hands in annoyance. "No, that's not what I'm worried about. I want to know how it is you happen to keep a gun in the house."

"An old habit."

"Left over from when?" she persisted.

"My previous occupation," he admitted.

"Which was what?"

"Talk about being grilled," Gray complained. "You'd make a good interrogator."

She ignored that. "You and Mitch worked together, didn't you? Just what kind of firm was it?"

Gray shrugged. "A big multinational. We were in charge of security. Mitch and I worked as a team until about five years ago. Then we bought each other a drink one night and decided we'd had enough. It was obvious there was more money and a lot less stress working on the business side rather than on the security side. We both had reasonably sound educations. We'd both had opportunities to observe the way some of the best businessmen in the world operated. We were tired of hopping from one trouble spot to another. We handed in our resignations and came home to spend the rest of our lives making money in dull, plodding, boring ways."

Amber's eyes softened. "You mean you hung up your guns and came home to lead a normal life. Just like a professional gunslinger in the Old West trying to live down his past."

Gray cocked one brow. "I think that may be over-dramatizing things a bit."

"Not in the least. I understand perfectly now."

"You do?"

"Of course. I haven't read all that Twitchell for nothing. No wonder all those gunfighter ballads appeal to you. Twitchell was always writing tales of men who had lived by the gun but longed for peace and quiet."

"I didn't exactly live by the gun, Amber. I had a good job with fringe benefits and a retirement plan."

Amber waved that aside with an airy gesture. "Nonsense. It was obviously the modern-day equivalent of the life of a gunfighter in the Old West. You must have had a good laugh that night I came to your rescue in Tucson. You didn't need me at all, did you?"

"I needed you," he stated with grave certainty. "I'll always need you."

She looked at him searchingly. "You're happy with your new life?"

He smiled slowly, watching her determined face. "Very happy."

"Excellent. Then that solves one problem." She was quite satisfied with his response.

"What problem?"

"Well, I certainly wouldn't want to have to worry about whether you might someday decide to take up you old career."

"You're happy being the wife of a dull, plodding businessman?"

"Very happy," she confirmed resolutely.

"Satisfied?"

"Quite satisfied."

"Content, even?" he ventured.

She shot him a quick, suspicious glare. "Very content."

There was a brief, curious silence as Gray continued to watch her. Then he calmly reached out and picked up the leather-and-brass volume of *Cactus and Guns*. Amber held her breath when he opened it to the fly-leaf.

"According to what you've written here, you're a little more than just content, Amber," he said softly. His eyes were almost gold.

She remembered every word of what she had written. It had been a very simple message. *To Gray, with all my heart and all my love forever. Amber.* "It was supposed to be a surprise," she whispered.

"Which? The book or the inscription?"

"The book." She glanced at the volume cradled in his big hands. "The inscription just sort of wrote itself."

"Did you mean what you wrote?"

Her eyes flew to his. "Every word," she said simply. "I don't think I'd allowed myself to really admit it until I saw what I had written. Then I knew for certain just what had happened. I love you, Gray."

He put the book down beside him and got to his feet. Amber smiled tremulously as he crossed the short distance between them. His hands closed over her shoulders. "I'm glad," he said quietly. "Because I love you very much, Amber Langley Grayson. More than I've ever loved anyone or anything in my whole life. And I'm going to go on loving you for as long as I live. You're a part of me. You became a part of me that day you knocked on my door and said the secretarial agency had sent you."

"I suppose I should have been suspicious about just why you kept me on after you discovered my typing wasn't exactly phenomenal. I told myself you admired my business sense."

"I did. I still do. But I sure as hell wouldn't have married you for it." He grinned wickedly and kissed her with a lingering warmth. "I've always considered myself a patient man, but there have been times during the past few months when I wanted to push things along a lot faster than they seemed to be going on their own. I decided if we got married you might start waking up more rapidly."

"Waking up?"

He nodded. "I thought of you as a very passionate Sleeping Beauty. I wanted to be damn sure I was the first man you saw when you came out of your protective daze. Possession being nine-tenths of the law, I decided to take steps to ensure I was the man in possession."

She shook her head in amused wonder. "I don't recall putting up much of an argument against the marriage."

"No, you just gave me a load of nonsense about not being the passionate type and then proceeded to seduce me on our honeymoon."

Amber blushed and laughed softly as she leaned her head on his shoulder. "I told myself I just wanted things to be normal between us. After all, we *were* married. I started getting very desperate when it became obvious you weren't interested in exercising your, uh, conjugal rights."

"I was interested in taking you to bed the moment I met you," he told her bluntly. "But I wanted you to want me, really want me. I didn't want you telling yourself you were merely carrying out your wifely duties. So I stalled until you finally took the initiative. After the first night with you in Phoenix, I realized I'd been wasting a lot of time for no good reason. You were every bit as passionate and giving as I'd dreamed. You had to be in love with me, I decided. It was just a matter of time before you woke up and admitted it."

Amber tightened her arms around his waist. "I'm sorry I took so long admitting it."

He chuckled into her hair. "It's all right. I haven't been feeling too deprived, although I wanted to shake you every time you used the word 'content' to describe your feelings."

"But I am content with you, Gray. Infinitely content. I can't imagine wanting anything or anyone else as long as I have you. I love you passionately, but I don't think pure passion has much chance of survival if there isn't an underlying structure of happiness and contentment. I've been afraid to admit the passion and love I felt for you because in the past those emotions proved very destructive. But now I know they work beautifully when they're based on other, more solid emotions." She lifted her head to meet his gleaming gaze. "In fact, the combination is dynamite."

"I know. I've been infinitely content with you, too, sweetheart. The main difference between us is that I wasn't afraid to acknowledge that the passion was there right from the start."

"Are we going to stand here all night and argue about who succumbed first to passion?" Amber laughed up at him with her eyes.

Gray's hands were strong and firm on her waist as he pulled her more tightly against him. The flare of male hunger in him was deepening the gold of his eyes. "I'd much rather succumb to passion than argue about it."

"Umm. There's just one more thing, Gray." She tried to hold him off a moment longer.

"What's that?" He was already nuzzling the nape of her neck, his breath warm and exciting on her skin.

"I want your word of honor that you won't ever, *ever* pack me off again the way you did yesterday just to get me out of the vicinity while you deal with the rough stuff."

"I should have known better than to try. You didn't waste much time heading right back here, did you? Just like a little homing pigeon."

"I would never have let you get me on that plane in the first place if I hadn't been so crushed and dazed by the fact that you actually thought I'd be stupid enough to go off with Roarke. That hurt, Gray."

He groaned and hugged her. "I'm sorry, honey. It was the only excuse I could think of to get you out of town."

"You should have told me the truth about Roger and Ozzie."

"I didn't dare. I knew for certain you'd never leave if you knew they were making trouble. I just needed a couple of days. I knew they'd make their move quickly. I wanted to give them enough rope so that they'd hang themselves, which they very obligingly did."

"Amateurs."

He laughed softly. "Exactly."

"I overheard Mitch talking to you on the phone late last night. That's when I knew there was something really big going on down here. I suppose Roger and Ozzie seemed like amateurs to you because of some of the types you'd dealt with back when you were in the security business."

"Roger and Ozzie are just a couple of small-time punks. Not very bright."

"What about Delaney?" Amber asked.

"I told the cops about him tonight, and they'll discuss the matter with Tucson, but I wouldn't be surprised if Delaney's on his way out of the country by now. Probably taking whatever cash was in the resort safe with him."

"I hope they catch him."

Gray shrugged. "They might. Roger and Ozzie will undoubtedly implicate him immediately."

"About this business of you pretending to be jealous of Roarke," Amber said, returning determinedly to the issue she had just raised.

"I wasn't exactly pretending. I was jealous as hell."

Amber's head came up abruptly. "I don't believe it."

"Don't get me wrong. I knew you weren't really thinking of running off with him. I knew you were committed to our marriage. But masculine jealousy is a rather primitive emotion. It doesn't always respond to logic. Just ask any man. Why do you think I told you to let Kelley in tonight when he just happened to show up at our door? I freely admit I wasn't above letting him see me with a gun in my hand and two victims in front of me, one of whom was conveniently sprawled on the floor."

Amber giggled. "Just like an ex-gunslinger to rely on his reputation to scare off a rival. But he was never a rival, Gray. When I left Southern California I never wanted to see him again. Even if I had never met you I wouldn't have changed my mind about Roarke. Once

I accepted the fact that he was a shallow bastard, nothing could have made me find him interesting a second time."

"Good," Gray said with deep satisfaction. "Then we won't mention him again."

"Suits me. Now can we go to bed?"

"Where did you ever get the idea you weren't sexy as hell, Mrs. Grayson?" Gray said admiringly. "Every time I turn around you're trying to drag me off to bed."

"Any objections?"

"None," he assured her. He scooped her up with ease and started down the hall to the bedroom.

Amber clung to him, her head on his shoulder as she reveled in the tender strength that surrounded her. When Gray stood her on her feet and began to undress her, she eagerly returned the favor. Soft laughter and teasing caresses turned quickly into passionate sighs and small cries of excitement and delight. Their clothing wound up in a heap on the floor.

Gray tumbled Amber down onto the bed, coming after her quickly to recapture her in his arms. His lips touched the hardening peaks of her breasts and his hands moved eagerly down her body to find the soft silk of her inner thighs.

Amber gasped as the passion flowered between them with an intensity that was as shattering as it was satisfying. For the first time she gave voice to the words that she knew now had been buried deep within her heart for weeks.

"I love you, Gray. I love you so much."

He drank the precious sounds from her lips and repeated them back to her as he joined their bodies with one swift, soft thrust. "My God, how I love you, Amber. I'll always love you."

The night spun a warm cocoon around the occupants of the wide bed, wrapping Amber and her husband in a passion that sprang from real love and a genuine contentment that would last a lifetime. Amber surrendered to the sizzling rapture, and Gray gave himself just as freely to the enthralling emotions that gripped them both. And when it was over they feel asleep in each other's arms.

THE SECOND FEISTY LETTER from Honoria Tyler Abercrombie arrived a few days later. Amber spotted it immediately in the morning mail and called out to Gray, who was in the kitchen making tea.

"Your nemesis, Ms Abercrombie, has struck again." She waved the letter at him in triumph as he sauntered back into the office.

"Is that right? What does she want to argue about this time?"

Amber eagerly scanned the contents of the letter. "She says she intends to go toe-to-toe with you in print over the matter of your interpretation of the last two stanzas of 'The Ballad of Billy Ballantine.' She's going to make you admit that the lines dealing with Billy's shootout with Big Jack Bonner are indeed sexual metaphors and that Twitchell had sex on the brain in almost every poem he wrote. Furthermore, he severely distorted history. According to her research, Ballantine never met up with Bonner in Texas or anywhere else."

"Hah. I can prove he did. There are newspaper accounts of the event. Ms Abercrombie's in dangerous territory now. Twitchell may have taken a few liberties with the truth, which was certainly his right as a poet. But he never distorted history to the extent of faking an entire shootout. Who does Ms Abercrombie think she is to say the last two stanzas of 'Billy Ballantine' are mere sexual metaphor? What kind of sex, anyway? It wasn't Twitchell who had sex on the brain, it's Honoria Tyler Abercrombie. She's undoubtedly a frustrated woman as well as a frustrated poet."

Amber was suddenly incensed. "That's not true! How dare you say that! Typical of a man to fall back on that sort of criticism when he can't find any real literary counterarguments."

"You want to bet Honoria Abercrombie is an eighty-year-old lady who gets her kicks out of arguing with me?"

"You're just jealous because she's got a copy of the *Collected Works*," Amber announced. "Maybe she has a copy of *Cactus and Guns*, too." Her eyes lit up. "Wouldn't that be something? Better hurry and write your article authenticating those poems as Twitchell's, or she's liable to beat you into print."

Gray smiled deliberately. "She'd better not try to beat me into print with an article on *Cactus and Guns*."

"Oh, really?" Amber sniffed. "Why shouldn't she? There wouldn't be much you could do about it except go through the roof."

"Don't count on it. If Ms Abercrombie provokes me too far, I might be tempted to teach her a thing or two about the proper use of sexual metaphor."

There was a beat of absolute silence in the room. Amber blinked slowly. "What exactly do you mean by that, Cormick Grayson?"

"I mean, Ms Honoria Tyler Abercrombie, that if you have any common sense at all, you won't dare try to scoop me with an article on *Cactus and Guns*. You haven't seen anything until you've seen the world's only legitimate Twitchell scholar explode."

Amber continued to stare at him for a long moment and then she collapsed back into her chair with a sigh of amused resignation. "How long have you known?"

"That you were Honoria Tyler Abercrombie?" Gray leaned back in his chair, steepling his fingers and gazing thoughtfully at the ceiling as he considered the question. "From the beginning, of course."

"Impossible! I covered my tracks too well. You couldn't have known. I had the letters forwarded from the publisher so they wouldn't have a local postmark. I made sure the article that got published mentioned that Honoria was from another state. *You couldn't have known.*"

"Never underestimate the intelligence of your employer, Amber. He may be slow at times, but he's not stupid." Gray was showing his teeth in a very masculine grin. "It was all the emphasis on big irons and smoking guns that gave you away. You were a little too determined to support Ms Abercrombie's point of view. If you want to know the truth, it gave me hope. I figured you wouldn't be so interested in the subject of poetic sexual metaphor if you weren't also somewhat interested in sex. Specifically, sex with me."

Amber grinned unabashedly. "I give up. I admit I couldn't resist creating Ms Abercrombie. I had a lot of fun with her. What's more, I think I shall go on having fun writing pedantic little articles arguing about Sherborne Ulysses Twitchell. You've had the field to yourself far too long. A little competition will be good for you. It will further the cause of Twitchell scholarship, if that isn't too much of a contradiction in terms."

"I shall look forward to your next article, Ms Abercrombie," Gray said with a gravely polite inclination of his head. He got to his feet and came around the corner of the desk. "In the meantime, I think we should explore your theories of Twitchell's use of sexual metaphor."

"Explore them where?" she asked demurely. "In print?"

"No, in the bedroom."

"Never let it be said," Amber murmured as she went happily into his arms, "that I'm not always ready and willing to meet the stringent demands of sound literary scholarship."

She allowed her poetically inclined ex-gunslinger to lead her off to bed.

# *Harlequin Temptation*

## COMING NEXT MONTH

### #129 FOR THE LOVE OF MIKE
**Candace Schuler**

Hired to chauffeur sexy Devlin Wingate, Michaelann wasn't about to accept his dinner invitation or get intimately involved. But what could she say when he popped the most important question of all?

### #130 THE REAL THING Barbara Delinsky

Within weeks Neil and Deirdre went from being total strangers to volatile roommates. Their love affair, however, had only just begun....

### #131 THE PERFECT MIX Cara McLean

Aubrey needed a bodyguard for her purebred cat. Robert came to her rescue. But what he excited in her went far beyond gratitude....

### #132 FOR ALL TIME Anne Shorr

Callie was determined to lambaste hotshot developer Michael Brookstone in her newspaper. Until he convinced her they should make love, not war....

# Janet Dailey
## Americana

Don't miss a single title from this great collection. The first eight titles have already been published. Complete and mail this coupon today to order books you may have missed.

**Harlequin Reader Service**

*In U.S.A.*
901 Fuhrmann Blvd.
P.O. Box 1397
Buffalo, N.Y. 14140

*In Canada*
P.O. Box 2800
Postal Station A
5170 Yonge Street
Willowdale, Ont. M2N 6J3

Please send me the following titles from the Janet Dailey Americana Collection. I am enclosing a check or money order for $2.75 for each book ordered, plus 75¢ for postage and handling.

| | | |
|---|---|---|
| _____ | ALABAMA | Dangerous Masquerade |
| _____ | ALASKA | Northern Magic |
| _____ | ARIZONA | Sonora Sundown |
| _____ | ARKANSAS | Valley of the Vapours |
| _____ | CALIFORNIA | Fire and Ice |
| _____ | COLORADO | After the Storm |
| _____ | CONNECTICUT | Difficult Decision |
| _____ | DELAWARE | The Matchmakers |

Number of titles checked @ $2.75 each =     $_____

N.Y. RESIDENTS ADD
  APPROPRIATE SALES TAX     $_____

Postage and Handling     $  .75____

                TOTAL     $_____

I enclose _____

(Please send check or money order. We cannot be responsible for cash sent through the mail.)

PLEASE PRINT

NAME _____

ADDRESS _____

CITY _____

STATE/PROV. _____

BLJD-A-1